ZANU

ZANU

Carol Matas

Fifth House

Saskatoon, Saskatchewan

1986

Canadian Cataloguing in Publication Data
Matas, Carol, 1949-
Zanu
ISBN 0-920079-27-X
I. Title.
PS8576.A72F6 1986   jC813'.54   C86-098023-5
PZ7.M37 Fo 1986

The author wishes to thank the Manitoba Arts Council for
their financial support. Also love and thanks to George
Szanto for his invaluable critiques. Any many thanks to
Caroline Heath for her detailed and meticulous
editorial work.

This book has been published with the assistance of the
Saskatchewan Arts Board
Canada Council

Published by
Fifth House, 406 Clarence Ave. S., Saskatoon, Saskatchewan
S7H 2C7

Typeset by
Apex Design Graphics, Saskatoon, Saskatchewan

Printed by
Gagné Printing, Louiseville, Quebec

Cover by Sarie Jenkins

To my son,
Aaron

CHAPTER ONE
Apparitions

Rebecca lay on her back, the lush grass tickling her neck and legs. She gazed up through the deep green leaves of the maple tree, to the clear blue sky. The leaves shimmered in the sunlight. She sighed with delight. There is nothing more beautiful in the whole world, she thought, than the green of the leaves and the blue of the sky, one against the other. The leaves and branches made intricate patterns against the blue. Two birds called to each other through the silence. O-can-a. O-can-a.

Rebecca was alone in the small clearing for a few blissful minutes. Everyone else had wanted to go for ice cream. She had begged off.

It was the annual picnic at Assiniboine Park. Her parents and their friends, a group that had been together since high school, assembled once every summer to eat food, run races, and pull as many muscles as possible. Naturally, 'The Gang' as they affectionately called themselves, saw each other often during the year. But this was a chance to see each other's children as well.

The kids had to go, of course, and it really wasn't too bad, Rebecca admitted. Except for the races. There was nothing she hated more than that awful moment between 'Get-set' and 'Go.'

Slowly Rebecca sat up, and rested her back against the tree. Perhaps she should catch up with the others—a fudgesicle wouldn't be such a . . . "Oh!" she exclaimed out loud. Standing directly in front of her, where a moment before had been nothing, was a boy, or rather, it seemed to her, an apparition.

Rebecca's first impression was of a mad glow of colour. The boy's hair was bright red, his face an almost shocking white, his eyes a deep green. He wore a long silky top which flowed almost to his knees, the sleeves puffed around the shoulder, then tight from elbow to wrist; and silky pants which clung like tights and were tucked into soft suede silver boots. Reds, greens, blues and yellows shot across the fabric in a jagged lightning design.

For a brief moment their eyes met—his desperate, shocked and, was it defiant?—hers astonished. Rebecca couldn't imagine why he should be shocked. He was the strange one, she was quite ordinary—a 12-year-old girl with short brown hair, high cheekbones and big brown eyes, dressed in red shorts and red and white T-shirt. He opened his mouth as if to speak, then closed it, looked around, turned and fled. Within seconds he had disappeared through the willows that surrounded the clearing.

For a moment, Rebecca sat, too stunned to move. Then she jumped up. Had she imagined it? Or had someone really appeared right in front of her?

"Oh my gosh," she murmured. For again, directly in front of her, this time unmistakably coming from nowhere that she could see, was another boy. He, too, looked desperate. He had light brown hair and light brown eyes; his face was round, pleasant. His mouth was set in a determined line. His clothes were the same style as the other boy's—only the colours differed. His top was gold, the tight pants lime green. He wore gold suede boots and a lime green beret.

He looked around and almost at the same time blurted out, "Was there someone else here just now? Red hair, about my age . . . ?"

Rebecca was shocked to hear him speak. After all, apparitions don't talk!

"Uh, uh," she stammered, "y-es, yes, I saw him. He appeared, just like you, out of nowhere. What is this? What's going on? You both appeared right out of nowhere!"

"Which way did he go?" asked the boy. "I *can't* lose him. I can't. You must tell me!"

Rebecca pointed at the spot where she'd seen the other boy disappear.

"Thank you," called the boy over his shoulder, already running through the willows where Rebecca was pointing. "Thank you so much."

Rebecca stood there for a moment, not moving, trying to convince herself she'd imagined the whole thing. On the other hand . . . her curiosity took over.

She darted through the trees. She could still see both boys. The first boy was halfway across a large grassy field, the second had only run about 100 metres. Rebecca, although she hated racing, always won the 100 metre dash. She suspected she could catch the boy if she wanted to. She stopped for a moment.

Maybe they're filming a movie here, she thought. And that's why they're wearing such weird clothes. Or they play practical jokes on people—and I'm chump no. 1. No, they both seem too serious for this to be a joke.

She couldn't stand it. She was burning with curiosity. She sprinted after the second boy. She was gaining on him rapidly when he glanced over his shoulder and saw her.

"I see him!" he called. "It's all right, I can find him, thank you!"

Rebecca just waved and smiled. She didn't stop but she slowed her pace to a jog. Polite, she thought, very polite. Nice way to say get lost, but he can't make me stop. I've got to find out what this is all about.

The boy glanced at her over his shoulder a number of times as he ran along. He tried to put on more speed, but Rebecca had no trouble keeping up; in fact, she had to force herself to stay behind him.

Then the first boy disappeared behind some trees. Rebecca knew the trees surrounded a duck pond, a large pond used for skaters in the winter, ducks in the summer. Soon the second boy was also behind the trees. Rebecca put on some speed and raced through the trees. She had to pull herself up short, for not more than thirty metres away the second boy was stalking the first. The redhead was leaning on the railing which surrounded the pond and staring, as if hypnotized, at the ducks.

The other boy waited a moment, then spoke very softly, "Jonathon."

Jonathon whirled around.

"Hi," said the other boy.

"Mark!" exclaimed Jonathon, obviously shocked. "How did you find me?" He paused. "And why?"

"You can't stay here," said Mark firmly. "I've come to get you. You don't know what effect you'd have. Think about it, Jonathon. One person. Little things you do could change other little things, those could add up to big things—and then we, at home, might not even exist. Do you know how dangerous it is for you to be here, unsupervised?"

Jonathon nodded his head, his eyes shining.

"Yes," he said. "I know. It's a wild chance. Maybe my being here will change everything. I know it's unlikely. But it's possible. It's possible. I'm going to stay!"

Rebecca stood, listening. What they were saying was so strange, she felt she was listening to a foreign language. None of this made any sense.

"You shouldn't have come," said Jonathon. "Now you'll have to stay too."

"No, Jonathon," said Mark urgently. "I don't have to stay and neither do you. Look, I know how you feel, but—but you have to come back—you'll be lost here—no one to take care of you—it's so different here—you won't make it on your own—if we go back now—no one will know the difference. I don't think they've discovered us missing yet. We can still go back!"

"And if they have?" asked Jonathon. "Then what? You know what'll happen to us," he said bitterly. "To both of us. Anyway," he added, looking almost cheerful for a moment, "we can't get back now."

Mark walked over to him and held out his hand. Cupped in the palm of his hand was a small, shiny black box. There seemed to be small red lights shining inside it.

"Wh—Wh—What did you do that for?" Jonathon shouted. "You know they only have to activate that—they can trace us now—"

"But we can get back with it!" Mark countered.

Rebecca had to see that box. What on earth was it? She decided it was time for the direct approach. She walked up to the boys.

"Get away from us!" Jonathon shouted as she approached.

Maybe he's crazy, thought Rebecca, or they both are. She was right beside them now. Maybe I'm a bit *too* close.

"Listen," Mark said to Rebecca, "please leave us alone. This is private. It's nothing to do with you. Please—"

"I'm sorry," she said, finally embarrassed, realizing how rude she'd been, standing right beside them, listening openly to their conversation. "I'm really—"

She was about to repeat how sorry she was, but she never got to finish her sentence. For in between "really" and the word that was about to come out, the world went soft. Or that's what it felt like to Rebecca. And when it hardened again she was no longer in Assiniboine Park. There were no birds singing, no grass, no trees, no duck pond. For a split second she felt a gut-wrenching fear that she, too, would soften and disappear. In an irrational gesture she grabbed each of her arms with the opposite hand and held herself tight, as if she could hold herself together. Her eyes were seeing something, but her mind, reeling from shock, was not processing the information. What her eyes saw was this: She was standing, with Jonathon and Mark, in a small round structure, about fifteen metres at the top, and large enough across for three adults to just fit comfortably.

"Mark," cried Jonathon, tears in his eyes, "what have you done?"

Just then part of the wall seemed to slide up and a large opening appeared. Four tall, very large men burst in through this opening.

Rebecca's main impression was that of boots—shiny black leather boots which reached up the whole leg. When she looked further she just saw more black—black shirts and black helmets. Tinted black plastic visors covered their faces.

"What's happened?" Rebecca screamed. "Where am I?"

She grabbed Mark's hand. "What's happened?"
He looked at her. His eyes seemed filled with pity.
"Whoever you are," he said, "I'm sorry, I'm very sorry—"

CHAPTER TWO
All Too Real

Rebecca was being pushed and there was nothing Rebecca hated more than someone pushing her around.

"Stop it," she protested. "Cut it out! You don't have to push me. I can walk!"

But the large, silent man, dressed in black, ignored her protests. A knot of fear had formed in the pit of her stomach and sat there like an iron ball. She yelled even louder because of it, trying to appear in control.

"Big bully! Jerk! Get your kicks picking on people a quarter your size, do you?"

What had happened? Was she dreaming? Perhaps when she lay down in that clearing she'd fallen asleep and was still dreaming. After all, she'd had dreams in which she dreamt that she'd woken up and described her previous dream to someone. And she'd really believed she was awake. Until she woke up. But if this was a dream, why couldn't she wake up? Wake up, she ordered herself. Wake up. But the dream continued. And it felt real. Very real. One minute in the park—the next . . . But those boys. They knew. It had something to do with that little box. The boys were being pushed by other guards just behind her.

She tried to look around, get her bearings, but it was very difficult. Every time she tried to focus on her surroundings she was roughly pushed forward again. She had the impression she was inside a large building, which seemed to be filled with displays behind glass. She caught a glimpse of shining cars, of all vintages, mannequins dressed in clothes of every description, some going back to at least the turn of the 20th century. There were machines of all sorts—toasters, vacuum cleaners, food processors. An entire room was filled with computers. Another with robots. Through these rooms, groups of children, and some adults, were being escorted by what seemed to be tour guides. Rebecca couldn't catch what was being said, and was too busy looking at the people to really care. Everyone was dressed in the most amazing fashion! Long robes, flowing pants, pleated silk shirts, hats, boots, flowers, feathers, and furs. Rebecca had never seen such a display of colour and design.

Suddenly she was outside, standing at the top of about fifty shiny silver steps. All around her, buildings shot up into the air. Tall, needle-like, they seemed at least a hundred stories high. Some were gold, others silver, many black. All shone with tinted glass, which reflected the sun and sky.

The sky was a strange colour.

It was more grey than blue, and yet there were no clouds. And the sun, although it shone in the cloudless sky, seemed dim. The air appeared clear, although it didn't have that clean, crisp prairie feel. The temperature was mild, perhaps 20°C.

"Down those steps!" the guard shouted.

Rebecca glanced behind her, and saw Mark and Jonathon stumbling through the wide doors, pushed by guards.

"Move! Move!"

They all ran down the stairs and were shoved into a sleek, black vehicle. It had three rows of seats. Two guards sat in the front. The children sat in the middle. The other two guards sat in the back. As soon as they were seated, shoulder straps and lap straps whirred silently into place and snapped the kids tightly against the seats. Rebecca almost jumped out of her skin, and by the startled looks on Mark's and Jonathon's faces, she knew that she wasn't just buckled in for safety. The vehicle seemed to lift slightly off the ground, then float down the street. The traffic was heavy and they moved slowly.

Stores lined the streets. People poured in and out of them, seemingly in a frantic rush. It was quiet in the vehicle, all sound was blocked out, but just outside the car windows was a jumble of colour and commotion.

Rebecca looked at Jonathon. He sat quietly, but Rebecca sensed fury seeping out of every pore.

He glared at her, then at Mark.

She turned to Mark. "Where am I? Tell me where I am!"

Mark, whose face had turned ashen, shook his head.

"You're in Winnipeg," he murmured, "but, but, well, how can you understand," he said sympathetically.

"Try me!" she insisted. "I'm not as dumb as I look!"

Mark look at her with admiration.

"You surprise me," he said. "You really do. Most people in this situation would be in hysterics by now, or in a dead faint. But you're making jokes." He paused. "All right. I'll tell you." Choosing his words carefully he said, "You've travelled. In one instant you travelled from your park to here."

"Here!" she exclaimed. "Here! Where is here?"

"Quiet back there!" barked one of the guards. "No more talking!"

"I want to know where I am!" shouted Rebecca. "And I'll talk till someone tells me!"

She felt Mark's hand over hers. It was freezing cold.

"Later," he said quietly. "We'll talk about it later."

There was something honest in his manner, and something which told her it would be dangerous to pursue the question now. She sank back against the seat. She pulled her hand away from Mark's. She stared ahead.

The dashboard looks like a computer centre, she thought idly. Oh, don't tell me I'm going to start shaking. I mustn't show them I'm afraid.

She always shook when she was really terrified. She shook and her teeth chattered. Take deep breaths, she thought. In, out, in, out. She could feel herself relaxing just a bit. You've been in tight spots before. Just keep your head. There's an explanation for all this. And you'll soon find out—something. She was very good at giving herself pep talks.

The vehicle slowed down in front of one of the very tall buildings. The building shimmered gold and seemed to narrow into a point at least a hundred stories up. They turned into a short driveway. A large door at ground level rolled up and the vehicle drove into a white, bare room.

The door rolled down and Rebecca knew by the sinking sensation in her stomach that they were in an elevator. Then with a slight jar, they came to a stop.

Snap! The belts slid away. The doors of the vehicle opened.

"Out! Out!" barked the guards.

But none of them moved fast enough for the guards, so one by one a guard reached in and yanked them out. Then one guard grabbed Rebecca by the shoulder and pushed her forward. She stumbled and almost fell into Mark, who was just in front of her. Jonathon was just behind her.

"Move," the guard screamed at her. She tried to shake his hand off. But it clamped down heavily on her shoulder, the fingers digging into her flesh. "Move!"

Rebecca tried to get a good look at where she was as she was being mercilessly prodded ahead, but she could get only a quick impression. It seemed to be a huge, black room filled with black desks, row after row of them, with people dressed in black working at shiny black computers. She stumbled along, her guard hissing in her ear, "Move," his hand now on her back, pushing, always pushing. They crossed the entire room and reached a door which slid open to the side as they approached. Rebecca was given one final shove. She found herself standing in a small white room. It had one huge black plastic chair in it. Soon she, Mark and Jonathon had been hustled into a row in front of the chair. Their guards stood right behind them. Rebecca felt like stepping back and giving her guard a good kick but she tried to control herself. At least her anger over being pushed had made her forget some of her fear.

A small man, with a grey face and thin grey hair, came into the room. He wore a black uniform and his shirt was covered with red and gold medals. He sat down on the black chair.

"Do you know who I am?" the man said to them, speaking so softly they had to strain to hear him. Rebecca knew that trick. Teachers did it sometimes so the kids would really have to listen.

Mark and Jonathon shook their heads.

Rebecca stepped forward.

"I don't know who you are," she said, "I don't know where I am, I don't know anything. I want you to tell me," she continued, her voice breaking. "I want," and she paused, for tears were unexpectedly stinging her eyes. She took a deep breath. "I want to go home! Right now!"

The man looked at her coolly.

"I," he continued, as if she hadn't spoken, "am Chief of Police Lows, chief for this entire region. So. I want you to know that your fate is in my hands. Answer me correctly and truthfully and you will feel my fairness. We won't even contemplate the results of answering with a lie. Will we?" He looked at them mildly.

To Rebecca's surprise, Jonathon stepped forward.

"It was really my fault," he said, speaking in a clear and defiant voice, looking right at the police chief.

"And you are . . . ?" asked the chief.

"Jonathon Kobrin," he replied, "10037."

"His file," said the chief to one of the guards, who immediately left the room.

"Go on, Kobrin."

"I wanted to experience the past for myself."

"The past!" Rebecca exclaimed.

"The reality of what it was like to live in those days," continued Jonathon, ignoring her outburst. "Not on some controlled time trip, but . . . At any rate, I went, and my friend here . . ."

"Your name?" asked the chief, looking at Mark.

"Mark Simms, 99725," replied Mark, his voice shaking.

The chief gestured to another guard, who then left the room.

"And then Mark," continued Jonathon, "tried to save me. To bring me back and keep me out of trouble."

"And this person?" said the chief, looking at Rebecca.

"And she's from my trip," said Jonathon, this time looking at Rebecca with a very concerned expression.

"What!" exclaimed the chief, leaping from his chair.

"What do you mean she's from your trip?"

"She was standing with us when you brought us back," answered Jonathon. "I told her to go away, but she wouldn't listen!"

"What year was it?" the chief demanded.

"1986," answered Jonathon.

"What is going on?" Rebecca almost screamed. "I demand to know! Where am I?"

"Never mind that," the chief barked. "Get me Lotts," he ordered.

The last guard left. The chief paced up and down in such a fury that for a moment no one dared speak.

A young, thin man entered the room.

"Yes, sir," he said, "can I help you?"

"I want you to take this girl to the museum and send her back immediately. These boys were using the machine illegally and they brought her with them."

Lotts just stood there.

"I, I . . ."

"Well, what is it?" exploded the chief.

"I can't send her back just now, sir," answered Lotts. "The machine is malfunctioning at the moment, sir."

"Well, get it fixed!" hissed the chief. "No doubt they didn't work it quite correctly. I want her sent back!" he repeated to Lotts. "Now get busy. Don't worry," he said to Rebecca. "You'll be back home in no time. Now just be patient for a moment while I deal with these two."

"But—" objected Rebecca.

"Quiet!"

Rebecca, realizing that her fate was in the man's hands, decided for the moment to obey, to be quiet and see what she could learn. Her mind buzzed with Jonathon's phrase 'The Past.'

Just as the chief sat down, a guard entered with two files

in his hand. He handed them to the chief, who opened one and then the other.

He glanced up at the two boys; his gaze settled on Jonathon. "Had some trouble in your family, that so Kobrin? Not quite keeping up?"

Jonathon stared steadfastly ahead. He would not answer.

"It says here you haven't bought anything in over a month. Now, that's hardly patriotic is it? And your sister. Mmmm. Not good at all. Couldn't pay her rent. Cut loose two months ago."

"Where is she?" Jonathon cried, his voice anguished. "What have you done with her?"

The chief ignored him.

"Now, Mark, you, on the other hand, seem to be fulfilling your duty well. Good family. Rash of you to go after your friend. Very rash. Nevertheless, you'll see how fair we can be. You can go."

Mark just stood there.

"What?" he whispered.

"You can go," the chief repeated. "But no talk about this—do you understand?"

At that moment, Lotts re-entered.

"What is it?" asked the chief.

"Well, sir," said Lotts, hardly able to find his voice. "Well, sir, it's the machine. Won't be fixed for twenty-four hours at least, sir. I'm sorry, sir."

The chief looked at Rebecca.

"Twenty-four hours," he muttered. "Have to put you in a cell, I suppose."

"Look," Rebecca pleaded. "If I'm to be here for twenty-four hours you have to tell me where I am! Or, or, I'll go crazy!"

He looked at her analytically.

"Possible, I suppose. Yes, possible. However, you might

feel you've gone mad if I do tell you . . . Well, all right," he said. "You've been transported into the future."

Rebecca turned white.

"Yes," he continued, "the future. You're from 1986. This is 40 R.C.E."

"40 Wh—what?" stammered Rebecca.

At this the chief actually laughed, although to Rebecca's ears it sounded more like gears grinding. "Well, in your years it's 2080. But we live in 40 the year of the Real Corporate Era. It's been just forty years since we adopted a new calendar, symbolizing a new beginning! This boy," he said, pointing to Jonathon, "was using the time machine illegally when he travelled back to your time. His friend tried to save him. And you, you were in the wrong place, at the wrong time. I just hope your absence won't have any effect on our future. Twenty-four hours," he muttered, "shouldn't be noticed, shouldn't do any harm. I'll have to check the 1986 records. See if we can locate you, see if it could make a difference."

Rebecca felt quite giddy. Transported to the future! A time machine!

For a moment she almost laughed. I mean, two summers in a row—it seemed like some kind of a bizarre joke. Only last summer she'd been transported in a time machine into a future so deadly, so terrifying—but how could there be two futures? On the other hand, she certainly believed that time machines could and did exist. Yes, she thought, it's possible. It's all possible. This is probably all real and I'm in the future and they're going to put me in a cell by myself for twenty-four hours and I'll be crazy by the time they let me out!

"You can't leave me alone in a cell!" she exclaimed. "It's not right. I'll go nuts." She looked around the room desperately. Her eyes lighted on Mark. He looked at her with such concern and sympathy that she found herself saying, "Let me stay with Mark until you can send me home! He can tell me all about your world. I'll have someone to talk to. It'll help. I'm sure that would help."

The police chief seemed startled. Rebecca expected him to say no, but instead, after thinking for a moment, he agreed.

"All right," he said. "Why not? Can't send you back home crazy, can we? Don't want to do any damage to our past, in any way. Who knows what little things could change our present. And we wouldn't want our present changed, not for the world. Yes, all right. You take her home, Mark. Take good care of her. Check in with me. Show her how well the future has turned out. You'll like it," he said to Rebecca. "You'll be amazed to see how far we've come!"

"Thank you," said Rebecca. "Thank you."

"Yes, sir, thank you, sir," said Mark. He paused. "Sir, I'm sure Jonathon didn't mean . . ."

"Just forget Jonathon, now," the chief interrupted. "For your own good, forget him."

A quiet menace Rebecca heard in his voice sent a shiver up and down her spine.

Mark and Rebecca were escorted out of the room by two guards. At least this time we're not being pushed, thought Rebecca.

"Goodbye." Rebecca heard Jonathon's voice as the door slid shut behind them. Mark winced.

Within minutes they were back in the vehicle, being transported through a city Mark called Winnipeg, but it wasn't a Winnipeg Rebecca recognized at all.

CHAPTER THREE
2080 or 40 R.C.E.

Rebecca and Mark sat quietly in the rear seat of the vehicle. Rebecca had stopped shaking. In fact, she was beginning to feel excited. A chance to see 2080 with her very own eyes! Would anyone back home believe her? Lonney would. And Lewis and Catherine. Oh, *wait* 'til she told them! She glanced at Mark.

He was still white; he sat with his head cushioned against the seat, his eyes closed.

Rebecca looked out of the window. They seemed to be moving slowly out of the shopping area and into a residential area.

To Rebecca the buildings in the residential area looked strangely like teepees. They were three-storey, triangular structures, the wide angle facing the street, the narrow angle at the back. They were placed so close together they seemed to be connected. They were all a dull red. Oak, birch, maple and willow trees were in full leaf on boulevards and front lawns.

The grass was green and flowers bloomed everywhere. Rebecca noticed the buildings were beginning to get smaller. They were exactly the same shape and colour, only now they were about two storeys high. The traffic began to thin out and soon they were driving down a street with triangles not more than one storey high. They stopped.

The vehicle's door slid sideways. Rebecca noted that there didn't seem to be any regular doors here, the kind that open and shut, but somehow part of the wall, or in this case the side of a vehicle, would just slide up or sideways, and slide back into place when you had gone through. Rebecca wondered how it worked.

Mark climbed out.

"Come on," he said. "This is where I live."

Rebecca scrambled out after him and watched with relief as the black vehicle sped away. She looked at his house.

"Why is everything red?" asked Rebecca.

"Oh," said Mark, "colour is very important. Red is a warm colour. Everything inside is colour coded, too. Come in, please."

They walked down the narrow sidewalk to the triangular door. There were no steps. Mark placed his hand on a milky white square in the centre of the door. The square glowed red. Then the door slid open.

Rebecca followed Mark into the house, but stopped just inside the door, she was so struck by what she saw.

The large front wall was windowless but the two side walls which met at a point at the back of the house were both glass from floor to ceiling. Trees and flowers were planted in perfect symmetry on the outside grounds so that Rebecca felt she was looking at a masterful, enormous piece of art. The colours and patterns were breathtaking. The wall behind her was a soft sky blue. The floor was covered in thick beige carpet.

Along the glass walls ran long, low, clear sofas, with clear backs, so nothing marred the view. Rebecca walked over to one and touched it, expecting something hard like glass. But the material rippled and gave to her touch. Gingerly she sat down. The sofa moved slightly and then formed around the contours of her body. It felt smooth and cool. She grinned. She loved it.

In the centre of the room was a clear round table with four clear, round chairs. At one end of the blue front wall, next to the door, was a clear blue desk and chair with a computer on it. On the other side of the door there were a number of strange-looking machines. One was a tall, shiny, blue box; the other was also a shiny blue, but the box was short and square. The tall box stood on the floor, the short box on a blue counter beside it.

Mark was standing in front of the tall box. Rebecca, full of curiosity, walked over to join him. To her surprise, he spoke to the box.

"Two dinners, please, #137. And make it something a little special. I have a guest here."

"Right away, Mark," a nasal, male voice responded. "I'll just have to order from the General Store. We're all out."

Mark turned back to Rebecca. "Have a seat." He motioned to the chair and table in the centre of the room. "You are hungry, I hope?"

Rebecca shrugged, not knowing really.

"Wh—what *is* that?" she asked.

Mark looked at her in surprise.

"Oh, of course," he smiled. "You lived in such a primitive time, didn't you? That's my fridge. It's ordering food." Mark spoke slowly, as if he were explaining something to a three-year-old.

"Each block shares an underground complex which stores food, household items, etc. A door in the floor of the fridge will open and the food will be lifted onto the shelves by a robot arm. If it needs to be cooked, I put it in my stove." He pointed to the short square blue box.

"Your dinner is here, Mark," announced the voice in the fridge. "Tell stove it's menu #425."

"Tell stove yourself," retorted Mark. "Can't you see I have a guest? I'm busy."

"Oh, of course, Mark," replied the fridge. "I am sorry."

Mark shook his head and removed two silver trays from the fridge. He put them in the stove, and that seemed to activate the element—or whatever the lights inside it were. A strange aroma soon filled the room.

"But how can the fridge talk to the stove?" asked Rebecca.

"Oh, everything here is tied into a central computer. They just have to access each others' circuits."

"Amazing," said Rebecca.

Mark opened the stove, pulled out the trays and set them on the table. He removed the shiny silver cover and steam rose into the air. Rebecca wondered why he hadn't burnt his hands taking it from the oven. She touched the lid. Cool outside, hot inside.

"TV dinners!" she exclaimed. "Well, I can get this at home."

"Uh-uh," snorted Mark. "This wasn't frozen. We get everything fresh every day. It's packaged like that so it can be cooked efficiently."

"Oh," said Rebecca. She looked at the food before her. "What is it?"

"Ah, kelp steak, tofu, and carob cake for dessert. May as well enjoy it," he said quietly. "Soon we'll only be eating food pills."

"What?" asked Rebecca, who hadn't quite heard him.

"I said, what would you like to drink?" he answered in a loud voice.

"What do you have?" asked Rebecca, uncertainly.

"Coke?" suggested Mark.

Rebecca burst out laughing. "Some things never change, do they?" she said.

A knife and fork lay neatly in the tray and, underneath them, a serviette.

The food tasted very strange. The steak was salty and fishy, the texture of the tofu was a bit like jello and the cake looked like, but didn't taste like, a chocolate cake. Rebecca, willing to try anything, found herself eating hungrily after the first tentative mouthfuls, even though she didn't exactly enjoy the food. She found the tofu especially unpleasant because of its strange texture.

I just finished a huge picnic a few hours ago, she thought to herself. Why am I so hungry? But that picnic already seemed years ago.

"Where are your parents?" she asked Mark through a full mouth. "Working?"

"Yes," he nodded. "My mother commutes to Denver, my father to Paris. They're both travelling reps."

"Wow!" exclaimed Rebecca. "That's tough. Who takes care of you? A babysitter?"

"A what?" laughed Mark, genuinely amused. "A babysitter? I'm thirteen years old, hardly a baby."

"But surely you don't live here on your own, do you?" asked Rebecca, hardly able to imagine such a thing. After all, she was twelve, and her parents still wouldn't leave her home alone.

"Oh, no," laughed Mark. "I have Sam. Sam, come here, please."

Much to Rebecca's surprise, a small section of the floor right beside the table slid aside, revealing a set of steps leading to a lower floor. Up these steps climbed a gleaming blue robot about the size and build of Mark.

"Hello, Mark," said Sam. "Did you have a successful day?"

"Well, Sam. I didn't get much work done this afternoon. I had a very strange experience . . . and she is part of it." He gestured to Rebecca. "This is Rebecca, Sam. She comes from the year 1986. I was there."

"You were *where*, Mark? In 1986? I didn't realize you had a history class today."

"No, Sam, I didn't. Never mind. I'll tell you later."

"And this young person is *from* the past?"

"Yes, Sam, she is, and we're supposed to take care of her until the time machine is fixed and she can go back."

"Of course. I'll just clean up here. Perhaps you could squeeze an hour of work in, Mark? Wouldn't do at all to fall behind now, would it?"

"No, no, it certainly wouldn't," Mark agreed. "You're quite right, Sam. U-uh, Rebecca, would you mind if I did some work? It's awfully important."

"But," Rebecca said, very puzzled, "you don't work, do you? I mean, what about school! Don't you go to school?"

"Yes, of course I do," said Mark. "I go to school in the morning. And I work in the afternoons. Everyone over ten years old works. At sixteen I'll work full time."

"What do you do?" asked Rebecca.

"Why, what almost everyone does, of course," answered Mark. "I'm a salesperson. That's what my parents do, only their company likes a personal touch—so they travel. I work for a clothing company and I sell scarves. I have to sell to as many stores as possible, and I even do individual sales. I do it all from here," he continued, pointing to his computer.

He sat down in front of the computer and began to talk to it, quoting numbers, names of stores, quantities and styles of his product. The computer spoke back, and also put the material on the screen for him to verify.

Rebecca watched without saying a word, although she was bursting with questions.

Mark worked for about half an hour, then stopped, got up and stretched.

"Well, that will keep my head above water," he said, smiling broadly. "I just sold twenty thousand scarves to Continental Division 323."

"You look like you really enjoy doing that," remarked Rebecca.

"Oh, I do," said Mark. "And it's important to keep up. I have to pay rent, buy food, have to buy new clothes every day, new video tapes every week."

"What!" exclaimed Rebecca. "Stop! Are you serious? New clothes every day? My mother would kill me. And why would you have to pay for rent and food? You're just a kid."

"Oh," said Mark, "you live in a very primitive time—I've told you that. We *have* to buy every day. It's every citizen's duty. And we have to sell enough to make enough money so that we *can* buy. It's a great system, don't you think?"

"Does everyone sell?" asked Rebecca.

"Not the presidents or executives of companies," replied Mark, "but everyone else."

"Well, who makes the stuff?" asked Rebecca.

"Robots, of course," laughed Mark.

"Robots," mused Rebecca. "Can they do that?"

"Yes," Mark replied. "They run all the factories on their own. They even repair their own systems when they break down. Of course, people still do some of the programming, but often robots program other robots. Hey," he said, changing the subject, "want to go shopping with me? It's a beautiful day. And all the kids will be at the stores by now."

"But can't you just order everything on this computer?" asked Rebecca.

"Sure we can, but it doesn't look good on your record. You're supposed to get out, meet people, have fun. Wouldn't be good to be stuck in all day, would it? C'mon, I'll show you."

It seemed pretty strange to Rebecca that if you didn't go out and have fun it would be marked down on your record. She felt uncomfortable with the idea of every move a person made being recorded and looked at by men like Chief Lows. Mark seemed happy and content, though, so perhaps she was wrong. What she had to worry about now was the shopping.

Actually Rebecca hated shopping, and her mother had to drag her downtown. But she wanted to see everything she could.

"Oh," smiled Mark, "you'll like it here. It's not *that* different from your time. Just lots better."

"Uh, Mark, what about Jonathon?" said Rebecca, feeling badly that they were about to go out and have a great time when they didn't know what trouble Jonathon was in. "I guess he must be in big trouble. Why did he do what he did?"

Mark shook his head. "I don't know, really I don't. You see, we use that time machine for controlled trips to the past. We go in history class, but always in small groups with a trained instructor. We view the world before the coming of the new era. But it can never be used the way he used it. It was very dangerous."

"Why?" asked Rebecca. "Why was it so dangerous?"

"When we use it we're sure never to involve ourselves in any way in the time we're visiting. The instructor knows how to avoid all such situations. He or she is very carefully trained. No student is allowed to go before their eleventh birthday so we can be sure they understand their responsibilities. But Jonathon was there on his own, with no supervision and no knowledge about how his actions would affect the future. Perhaps some little thing he did would change some other little thing and so on and so on until in 100 or 200 years the changes would be quite large. Perhaps this world wouldn't exist like this at all— and," he muttered, very much to himself, "at least we know what we're dealing with here. Who knows if a different future wouldn't be even worse."

"Even worse?" Rebecca repeated. "I thought you loved everything here."

Mark shot a quick glance at Rebecca, his soft brown eyes suddenly hard. Then he laughed. "But I do, I love it all. You must've misunderstood." And without stopping for breath, he went on. "Have you ever thought about what the future would be like?"

That question stopped Rebecca cold. She stared at Mark for a moment before she answered. What do I tell him, she thought to herself. That this isn't the first future I've seen? He's so—I don't know, like a school teacher almost. Who knows how he'd react. Probably think I'm crazy. And what I'd like to know is how can I be here, in the future, when I've seen the future and it's completely different. Could there be more than one future? Is that possible?

Rebecca chose her words carefully.

"I think of the future," she said, "all the time. And I hope we can affect the future. Do *you* think one person, like Jonathon," or, she thought, like Lewis, Cath, or even me, "could make a big difference, really change things?"

"Yes, I do think one person can change things," Mark replied.

"The future," he continued, "is not necessarily a straight line. In fact, perhaps it's more like a fan. Picture yourself at the fulcrum of a fan. The decisions you and the people around you make will propel you along one or another of the fan's strands. But then you arrive at another fulcrum, and another. So the future is made up of countless possibilities."

Countless possibilities, thought Rebecca. What an incredible idea. If she had a time machine in 1986 and programmed it for 2244 she could land up in thousands of endless different futures, perhaps a different one each trip.

Aloud she said, "And the things we do could eventually narrow the possibilities until finally we are in the future, or present, we have created. And perhaps, what one person does would move us into one future instead of another. What an idea."

"Maybe I should have left him," mused Mark, again to himself. "Maybe . . . "

"Oh, no! I'm sure you did the right thing," Rebecca tried to reassure him.

"Jonathon was my best friend, but he hasn't worked for a month. Just stopped. Is that any way to behave? What if everyone did that? He can't just drop his responsibilities like that. I tried to talk to him, to tell him. But it didn't do any good. Must run in the family." Mark shook his head.

"What did the chief mean, cut loose? What's going to happen to Jonathon?" asked Rebecca.

"I don't want to talk about it," Mark said, getting up in an abrupt motion, but Rebecca was sure she had seen sudden tears in his eyes.

"I'm sorry, Mark, we don't have to talk about it. I'm afraid some people just love to cause trouble. Still, it hurts when it's a friend, someone you thought you understood. I think you're great—trying to help him, going after him like that!"

"Yes," answered Mark. "But he was my best friend. What else could I do? Well, come on, let's go shopping."

Rebecca got up and followed Mark out the front door.

He led her around the house, down a beautiful path surrounded by flowers, into the back lane, where they got into a small, blue vehicle. He sat in the driver's seat. "This is my skimmer," Mark explained.

"You drive?" asked Rebecca, astounded.

"Of course," answered Mark, who seemed to have become more cheerful at the prospect of going shopping. "Everyone over ten drives and owns their own skimmer. That way more people buy vehicles. I buy a new one every six months. But by the time I'm twenty, I'll buy a new skimmer every week!"

"What do you do with the old ones?" asked Rebecca. "And your old clothes and stuff?"

Mark pointed to a small silver booth. Each house in the lane had one. To Rebecca it looked like a solid silver phone booth set neatly beside the carport right where the garbage cans would be if this were 1986. "It's a disintegrator," he said. "Don't walk into it by mistake," he laughed.

And with that, he activated the computer, the skimmer lifted off the ground, and they floated down the street.

CHAPTER FOUR
The Shopping Centre

"The first thing we have to do," answered Mark, "is buy *you* some clothes. Why, you'll stand out terribly in that outfit. It's so plain."

Rebecca glanced down at her red jogging shorts and T-shirt. She looked at Mark's gold silk top, his green pants, his suede boots.

"Yeah," she sighed, "I see what you mean. But I have no money."

"Never mind," said Mark. "After the sale I just made I can afford to buy one extra outfit. And it'll look good on my record. *Two* outfits in one day!"

"Your record?" said Rebecca.

She was just about to ask Mark to explain how these records worked when Mark, looking at the dash, exclaimed, "Oh, no! We forgot to check in!"

Quickly he pressed a small button on his dashboard. A voice spoke.

"Operator."

"Operator," said Mark, "please connect me with Chief of Police Lows. He's expecting me."

"One moment please."

"99725?"

"Hello, sir."

"What are you doing now, Mark?"

"We're going shopping, sir."

"Good, Mark, good. And Mark?"

"Yes, sir?"

"Don't forget to check in often. I want to know where you are at all times. I may have to bring you in quickly."

"Yes, sir. I will, sir."

"That's all. Sign off."

"Yes, sir. Signing off."

Mark turned to Rebecca with a weak smile. "That was close."

Rebecca looked at him quizzically.

"Would it really have mattered if you'd forgotten to report in?"

Mark laughed nervously.

"Of course it would! They won't tolerate mistakes or tardiness."

"They?"

"Yes, you know, the police, the company. Look over there. We're going to that shopping centre."

Traffic was quite heavy now, and they moved slowly towards a large vehicle park.

"Ah, we're in luck," Mark said, as he manoeuvered his skimmer into a just-emptied space. The skimmer sank to the ground and the doors opened.

"C'mon," he urged, his eyes shining. "We'll get you something really beautiful."

Rebecca and Mark walked through the lines of skimmers, across the smooth white surface of the vehicle park. People, all flamboyantly dressed, were hurrying into the shopping centre, or, laden with parcels, were rushing back to their skimmers. Rebecca looked with interest at the large, round, smooth white building with a green-domed roof. As she and Mark approached the building a door large enough for ten shoppers to enter at the same time slid up and open.

"Wow!" Rebecca said aloud as she and Mark walked through the door.

The area inside the building was the size of a football field, and was filled with light and colour. Fountains shot up into the air. The water was coloured, so the air was awash in rainbows. Surrounding the fountains were exotic trees. Some of them Rebecca could identify—orange, apple, lemon and grapefruit grew beside olive and cork trees. Palms swayed in a light breeze. Orchids, tiger lilies, mums and roses grew out of the cropped, green grass that covered the floor. And throughout this maze of colour and fragrance were hundreds of mannequins, each one dressed in a different, elaborate design.

The mannequins were posed in various postures—some leaning casually against a tree, some poised as if to run or dive or throw a ball, some picking flowers, others in conversation with each other. They looked so real it was hard to tell the mannequins from the shoppers.

Rebecca stood just inside the door, quite staggered by the sight.

Mark laughed. "Come! Pick any outfit you want. I'll buy it for you!"

Rebecca wandered through the building with Mark, but she had a hard time concentrating on shopping. The trees, flowers and fountains were so beautiful.

"How," she asked, "can a cork tree grow beside a fir? They need such different climates."

"They're all genetically engineered to grow under just these conditions," explained Mark. "The flowers, too, of course. Everything here is for sale," he chattered. "There's big business in landscaping. People have to change their flowers and trees at least once a month."

Rebecca stopped and stared at him.

"How can you change a tree?"

"Oh, it's easy," Mark answered. "We have machines that do all that, and special fertilizers that make the trees and flowers take immediately to their surroundings. I mean, you can't have a tree hanging 'round for hundreds of years. Or flowers regrowing every year. Where's the profit in that? Now choose an outfit."

Something was beginning to bother Rebecca, but she tried to concentrate on the task at hand.

"All the clothes are on the mannequins," Mark explained. "Find an outfit you like, then I'll show you how to order it."

"I like that top," said Rebecca, pointing to a bright red top which covered purple pants and gold lamée boots.

"You can't just get the top," Mark said. "All or nothing— even the boots are included."

"But that's not fair," Rebecca objected. "I only want the top. I'll find a different pair of pants."

"It's not a matter of fairness," Mark explained, stopping for a moment to deliver a small lecture, "it's a matter of profit. If you like the top, you have to buy all of the outfit, then you spend more money and it's better for everyone. You can always switch and wear it with a different pair of pants at home."

"Well, I think I'll pass on that one," said Rebecca, making a face. "Red and purple. Yuck."

The next one she saw was a brilliant orange top with short sleeves and short lime green pants.

"This is lovely," Mark suggested.

"No." Rebecca shook her head.

She stopped in front of a mannequin leaning gracefully against a lemon tree. It wore a pale yellow silk blouse with three-quarter sleeves which puffed just under the elbow. The blouse reached to just above the knee. There were soft yellow silk pants, which were worn tight, and tucked into short silver boots. A rainbow-coloured scarf was wound around the waist.

"That one," said Rebecca. "Please." And she had to admit to herself that although she normally hated shopping this was not so bad. In fact, she couldn't wait to try on that outfit. It really was spectacular.

Mark pressed some buttons on a small machine which had been built into the mannequin's palm and within minutes a silver robot appeared, bearing a box with her clothes in it.

"How do I know they'll fit?"

"Oh, they'll fit. Your size and measurements were taken the minute you walked through that door. Hey! There are some kids from my class at school! That robot will take you to the changing rooms. You get changed and come back out here and I'll introduce you."

The robot slid silently over the floor, weaving in and out among shoppers and displays with no effort. Rebecca hurried after it. In the centre of a cluster of giant apple trees was a small square structure covered in vines and ivy. A number of square pieces were leafless, and one of these slid up as the robot approached. The robot entered. Rebecca followed. They were in a large room, large enough for ten people to change in. Mirrors covered the walls from floor to ceiling. The floor was covered in thick purple carpet, at least three centimetres deep. Plush purple arm-chairs were placed carefully in the corners. The robot deposited the box on a long, clear purple table, then turned and left. The door slid shut. She was alone. Rebecca walked over to one of the chairs and sank down into it. She opened the box and stared at the clothes. She picked them up, touched them. They felt like nothing she had ever felt before. The silk was so fine, so pure, so smooth. The colour was the colour of the sun. Slowly, almost reluc-tantly, she took off her own clothes, her only, she felt, direct link with her real world. Soft cotton underwear and socks, all in yellow, lay on top of the silk shirt. She put these on first. Then the pants, the shirt, the boots.

She wound the scarf around her waist, and tied it in a knot at the front, the way she'd seen it done on the man-nequin. She stared at herself in the mirror. The material felt heavenly, smooth and cool, against her skin. It was real, very real, and for the first time since this whole series of events had started, she really believed it was happen-ing; she had landed in the future. And, she thought, in some ways quite a nice future. I've never been one for lots of clothes and things but everything here is *so* gorgeous. I don't suppose it hurts to live in this kind of . . . sump-tuousness. Yes, that seemed the right word. It was sump-tuous. Now how was she to get out of the dressing room? She walked to the door and, fortunately, it slid up.

The robot was waiting for her. It took her back to Mark and his friends. She had forgotten all about her old clothes—they remained in the changing room.

She was introduced to three kids, two boys and a girl. Mark told them she was a visitor from out of town.

They chattered on and on about their purchases and the new styles being introduced this week. Finally one of them asked where Jonathon was.

Mark shrugged.

"Haven't seen him. Not at school. Not at home."

The three kids glanced at each other and then shrugged too, as if silently agreeing not to mention Jonathon again.

I know he was probably rotten, thought Rebecca, but if they were his friends, it's sure strange they don't seem to care much about what's happening to him . . .

Mark decided it was time to leave and do some other shopping. They went back to Mark's skimmer and Mark took Rebecca downtown, to a dizzying round of shops. He bought two lighting fixtures, a chair, two video discs and a painting. Art work, too, he explained, had to be replaced, although you could keep a painting for as long as three weeks if you really liked it.

"Surely paintings don't go into the disintegrator too?" asked Rebecca.

"Of course," answered Mark. "Everything does. Otherwise we wouldn't need more of them, would we?"

All the shops were beautiful. It seemed to Rebecca that they used everything—fabrics, plants, stained glass—to enhance the pleasure of buying.

They were just walking out of a robot store, where Mark had been showing Rebecca all the latest models, when Rebecca saw a hand catch Mark's shoulder. She turned at the same time as Mark. The girl they saw was tall, about Rebecca's age. She had long, shocking red hair, deep blue eyes and pale, white skin.

"Where is he?"

"I don't know," muttered Mark, looking down.

"Mark, you're his best friend," she implored. "He's been taken, hasn't he? Cut loose? If you won't help him, who will? Tell me, please!" Tears sparkled in her eyes.

Mark shook his head, in a stubborn gesture.

"Forget it, Tara, forget it. Or all three of you will end up the same."

Then he grabbed Rebecca's hand and pulled her away. Rebecca looked back over her shoulder to see Tara standing helplessly in the middle of the street, people jostling her every which way. *She* doesn't look bad, Rebecca thought.

"Was that his sister?" she asked Mark as they hurried to the skimmer.

"Yes, and if she doesn't watch it, she'll end up the same as he has. I don't even want to be seen with her anymore. Contact with that family will go down bad on my record, I can see that now. I'll have to stop talking to her."

"But surely," Rebecca objected, "talking to someone can't hurt you. I mean . . . "

"Oh, please be quiet, Rebecca. We have to go back and check in. Hurry up."

Rebecca looked at Mark closely. A queer feeling was beginning in the pit of her stomach. She liked Mark. And she'd thought Jonathon a pretty rotten person for causing so much trouble. But was it that simple?

Back in the skimmer Mark called in. The machine was still malfunctioning. They were ordered to get some rest and check in the next morning.

They had eaten lunch late, at about two, so for dinner they just had kelp sandwiches and tofu cakes. As they were sitting at the table Rebecca said, "Does Jonathon's family live around here?"

"Yes, unfortunately," sighed Mark. "It'll be hard to avoid Tara. They live just four houses down the street. But it doesn't matter. I'm never going to visit that house again."

"But Mark, why not? I still don't understand. And what has happened to Jonathon? Does he have a lawyer to help

him? Maybe you should at least make sure he has a good
lawyer."

Mark stared at Rebecca as if she was talking in a foreign
tongue. One he had never heard.

"A lawyer," he repeated pensively. "A lawyer." He shook
his head.

"Rebecca, I think I'd better tell you a little bit about the
year 40 R.C.E. It is very different from 1986. I know. I've
been to 1986, you know, in history class. The world on the
brink of nuclear disaster, small wars everywhere, people
dying of every kind of disease, starvation. Crime, violence,
unemployment . . . Well, look around you. We live in a
paradise by comparison. No war, because there are no
countries left to fight each other . . .

"What!" exclaimed Rebecca. "What happened to Canada?
That police chief said this was still Winnipeg!"

"Oh, yes," said Mark. "The cities still have the same
names, but we all live and work for Zanu. Everyone in the
world does!"

"Zanu," repeated Rebecca. "Everyone in the world. I don't
understand. What is Zanu? Like the U.N.?"

Mark laughed. "No," he snorted, "Zanu is not like the
U.N.—that bunch of incompetents. Zanu is a corporation.
The only one left."

"A corporation? But how . . . ?"

"In the 80s," Mark was beginning another lesson, "big
business really started to come into its own. It ran the so-
called elected governments—no one dared oppose it. But
the governments could still cause trouble—starting wars,
East and West hating each other. Over the next few years,
though, the corporations became bigger and bigger until
there were only three or four. Finally, it was obvious that
the governments were just figureheads, so they were abol-
ished, and Zanu became the one and only corporation.

"Zanu labs produce medicines. Zanu mines the oceans for food and minerals, it builds our houses, it . . . well, it takes care of us. And as long as everybody works hard and sells, and contributes, it can keep on forever. Can you imagine what would happen if all of a sudden no one wanted to sell? Everything would fall apart. There'd be chaos. Maybe even war, like in your time. So you see . . . "

"And Jonathon wasn't buying, that's what the chief said . . . " Rebecca murmured. She was astonished by this news. An entire world—one big business.

"Yes," exclaimed Mark, "and if everyone stopped buying, it would be terrible. The whole system would collapse. We'd starve, we'd die. You see, we all have to be responsible. We have to keep buying."

"Well," said Rebecca, "I see what you mean . . . and from the sound of it things are a lot better than in our day. Still," he said, "you'd think there'd be a little room for someone who feels differently."

"No," said Mark. "There can't be. Unless we want chaos." With that he got up from the table.

"C'mon. I'll show you where you'll sleep tonight." And that was the end of the discussion.

CHAPTER FIVE
Tara

Mark stepped on a small red button on the floor. A piece of floor slid away, revealing steps.

"This way," he said. They walked down about ten carpet-covered steps. A hallway ran the length of the house, narrowing until both sides joined to form a door at the end. Directly to Rebecca's right was a door, and to the left was another one.

"This is my parents' room," Mark said as he pressed a small red button to the side of the door to the right. The door slid sideways and Mark walked in. "You can sleep here."

Rebecca followed him into a room shaped like a triangle cut in half. The long side was the side with the door. There was a large double bed in the front of the room. The long wall opposite, which slanted to a point at the back, was covered with mirrors. Beside the door on the left was a long, low, clear pink vanity table; beside the door on the right was a silver rack, with clothes hanging on it.

Mark pointed to the small red button just inside the room, on the wall beside the door. "Press this to open the door," he instructed. He looked over the rack of clothes, which was so full he could barely see what was there, and took down a long, shocking pink silk night dress. "It'll be long," he said, "but you'll manage, I'm sure. The bathroom is at the end of the hall. My room is across the hall—should you need anything, just let me know. I'll wake you in the morning. Have a good rest. Goodnight."

"Goodnight," replied Rebecca.

Mark smiled at Rebecca and walked out the door and across the hall to his room. Rebecca pressed the red button, the door slid closed. She looked around. The bed was covered in a bright pink satin cover, the floor carpeted in pale mauve. She inspected the vanity table. It was full of bottles, jars, tubes. She picked one up. 'Younga, skin cream for men,' the label said. She picked up a tube and opened it. White lipstick. She opened a jar labelled "Devastation." A very strong perfume. There was also deodorant, cosmetics, and coloured hair spray. She went over and looked at the clothes. She knew she shouldn't be snooping, but she couldn't help it. There were pants, blouses, suits, evening gowns and about fifty different pairs of boots and shoes. There was so much of everything, it was all so beautiful, so lavish, so—enthralling. But it almost made her dizzy. It seemed to her that after awhile, you would want more and more and more and more until you could think of nothing else.

She changed into the nightgown and lay down between the pale pink silk sheets, her head sinking into the floral-patterned down pillows.

But Rebecca couldn't sleep. She tossed and turned, she tried deep breathing. Nothing worked. Her mind was racing. A whole world run by one company. It was hard to believe. Still, perhaps it was the answer. Certainly, even in 1986, a lot of people thought business could solve the world's problems. Certainly the most important leader in the West thought so. Her class studied the newspapers for fifteen minutes every day, so she knew a bit about it. And if it was the answer to war, disease, poverty, well, how could it be wrong?

Still, a picture of Tara, standing in the middle of the street, haunted her. Of course, there would always be people who wanted to wreck everything . . . maybe Jonathon and Tara were like that. It made her think of her cousin Norman. Ugh. Yes, there were definitely people who needed to be disciplined! But *why* did something in the pit of her stomach feel . . . well . . .

Oh, I can't stand this, she thought, and she got out of bed. She put on her new clothes, then pressed the button to the bedroom door. It slid open. She climbed the stairs, the door sliding open as she reached the first floor. The large inner room was now dark, crowded with shapes and shadows. In fact, one shadow was moving toward her!

"What's that?" she cried out.

"It's Sam," said the robot. "Is there something I can do for you?"

"Uh, no Sam, I just can't sleep. Maybe some fresh air."

"But it is very late and you are not allowed on the streets after 12 o'clock."

"Oh, all right, Sam, I won't go on the street. I'll stay in the front yard, or right in front of the door if that makes you happy."

"Happy?" asked Sam. "It will not make me happy or unhappy. I do not experience such emotions. But yes, if you stay by the door I suppose that will be satisfactory."

"Thanks, Sam. Could you turn on a small lamp for me? Just so I can find the door?"

Sam did so and Rebecca crossed the room, pushed the button for the front door and let herself out into the night.

The temperature hadn't changed since the afternoon. The air was the same, too. It didn't have that fresh night smell. There was a faint smell of flowers.

Rebecca sat down on the grass and looked up at the sky. At home there was nothing she found more wonderful than sitting in her yard, looking up at the sky filled with stars. She'd find all the constellations she knew, make wishes, and drink in the beauty and peace of a still, clear night. But much to her surprise, here she could see no stars. There had been no clouds earlier. She sighed. She was beginning to feel homesick. What about her parents? They'd be worried, no doubt. What would they think when they got back from getting ice cream and she was gone. Vanished without a trace.

It was so quiet. There wasn't a soul out. And it was very dark. There were no street lamps. But wait, there was something. She could hear a dull hum.

A skimmer was driving slowly along the street, headlights dimmed. It passed her and continued down the street. Rebecca got up and crossed the lawn so she could see where the skimmer was going. She stood behind a large oak tree and watched. It was so dark that it was hard to tell what was happening. The skimmer stopped along the curb. She saw four large shapes get out of it. They moved up to one of the houses. She could hear a pounding on the door. It slid open and light momentarily flooded the scene.

She saw four police guards, all dressed in black, weapons drawn, standing at the door. She gasped. Then she saw an older man and woman step out of the house. They looked frightened. The woman was objecting, pointing back to the house. One of the police shook his head and roughly pushed the couple towards the skimmer. And then Rebecca saw Tara, and heard the woman call, "Go back in dear, please. Be good, don't worry. We'll be back soon!"

She heard Tara call, "Mother! Father!" And then saw a police guard turn and point a weapon directly at Tara.

Then Tara backed into the house and the door closed.

Blackness once again enveloped the scene, as if a movie projector had suddenly broken down. Rebecca saw the skimmer drive off.

She waited until it had completely disappeared into the blackness and then, without stopping to think about what she was doing, she ran, heart pounding, to Tara's house. She knocked softly on the door, looking around, afraid someone might be watching.

The door slid open. For a moment Tara was speechless.

"Wh—wh—who are you?" she stammered, her face streaked with tears. She seemed totally confused by Rebecca's presence. "I thought you were . . . Who are you?" she repeated.

"You thought it was the police again," said Rebecca. She looked at Tara's desolate expression and a rush of pity for Tara swept over her. "I saw the whole thing," Rebecca said. "Look, let me in. I don't want to be seen."

Tara, who appeared to be in shock, stepped aside and let Rebecca in.

Rebecca looked around. They were in a house very much like Mark's. They seemed to be alone.

"Is anyone else here?" she asked.

Tara shook her head. She was shaking.

"Well, I don't know what I'm doing here really," said Rebecca, suddenly realizing it herself. "It's just, I saw everything and, I don't know, I thought maybe you'd need help. Are you all by yourself?"

"Who *are* you?" repeated Tara, staring at Rebecca in bewilderment.

"Oh, I'm sorry. You don't remember me, do you? I was with Mark this afternoon when you stopped him. Guess you didn't really notice me . . ."

"No," said Tara. "I guess I didn't. I was thinking about something else."

"Yeah," said Rebecca, "I know. Look, you'd better sit down. You look awful. Do you have a blanket or something?"

Tara pointed to a long, low, beige sofa which ran along one wall. On it was thrown a large black silk shawl, with white fringes. Rebecca guided Tara over to the sofa, wrapped her in the shawl, then sat her down. Rebecca sat down beside her. Tara sat stiffly on the sofa. She was wearing short white pants which ballooned out and tightened just above the knee and a sleeveless blue silk shirt. She tried to fit her bare legs under the shawl by bringing her knees up to her chest and clutching the shawl tightly around her legs. She couldn't stop shaking.

"Tell me why they took your parents," said Rebecca. "I really want to know. And why did Jonathon do what he did?"

"What do you know about Jonathon?" asked Tara, sitting up straight. "Do you know something? And who are you? What are you doing here? Are you from Zanu?"

Rebecca shook her head.

"You're not?" Tara seemed to become alarmed.

"No," said Rebecca, "I definitely am not. My name is Rebecca, and . . ."

"Just a minute," whispered Tara. "Don't say anything more. If you aren't from Zanu you probably shouldn't be here. You'll get in trouble if they hear you."

"Hear me?" whispered Rebecca. "How?"

Tara pointed at the computer console in the centre of the room.

Rebecca looked at it in dismay.

"They can tune in on us whenever they want," Tara whispered, practically in Rebecca's ear, "and they might very well want to see if I do anything or contact anyone now that my parents are gone."

"How about outside?" whispered Rebecca. "Can they hear out there?"

Tara shook her head.

Rebecca motioned to Tara to turn off all the lights. Tara did so and quietly they let themselves out into the black night. Tara took Rebecca's hand and led her into the backyard. They crouched underneath a gigantic weeping willow.

"Look," Rebecca continued to whisper, "I might be able to tell you something about Jonathon, but first, you tell me what happened just now."

"You saw," answered Tara, her tears returning, "they came and took my parents."

"But where," asked Rebecca, "and why? And what will happen to them?"

"Why should I trust you?" asked Tara. "Why should I tell you? I don't know anything about you."

"Okay," sighed Rebecca. "I'll trust you first."

Somehow, in spite of what Mark had said, Rebecca liked Tara and had trusted her immediately. She decided to tell her the entire story. She began with her first glimpse of Jonathon as he appeared in the park and she told Tara everything right up to the moment Rebecca had witnessed the police raid.

Tara was still wrapped up in the shawl Rebecca had found for her and she listened, the shawl pulled tightly around her, her whole body shaking.

"It's unbelievable," she whispered to Rebecca, when

Rebecca had finished her story. "Do you really come from 1986?"

"Really," said Rebecca.

"But you seem like anyone else," said Tara. "I thought anyone from before R.C.E. would be . . . I don't know . . . well, sort of primitive. After all, look at the conditions you lived in."

Rebecca laughed. "Well, it's not that long ago. We're not exactly Neanderthals—although, on second thought, if you saw some of the kids in my class . . . " She giggled. Much to her surprise, Tara giggled, too.

"Yes," Tara said, "I know what you mean."

"Anyway," said Rebecca, "Mark seems to think you've got things pretty good here—although I sure don't like those police. Why did Jonathon do it?"

Once again Tara sighed. "I don't know if it's because they took Laura, or if he would have done it anyway. I think, you know, he would have anyway."

"Laura?"

"My oldest sister." Tara's voice was so low Rebecca could hardly catch the words. "She was supposed to leave school to work full time. But she wanted to stay in school! She wanted to study history. So they came to get her. They told us she would stay in school—but a different kind of school. 'Re-education' they called it. She'd learn what her real duties were, duties to Zanu. Then they'd let her come back. That was over a month ago. We haven't heard from her since."

"Then Jonathon, well, he just didn't fit. He liked to write stories, and draw. And he used to do that instead of working. He didn't pay much attention in school when he was being taught all about Zanu. Instead, he'd daydream, draw . . . I don't know. He hated shopping, he hated selling. He got hold of all sorts of books from the past, illegally. Books we aren't allowed to read. He'd swipe the micro chips from the history museum, then put them back before anyone realized they were gone. He would take incredible risks. He could've been caught anytime. I know he didn't like the world before Zanu. But he didn't like this one either. He always talked to me about being free — about having the right to live any way you wanted to. And you know," said Tara, her voice dropping even lower, if that was possible, "I agree with him. It's true, we don't want war and crime and disease. But that doesn't mean we have to have this. Anyone who doesn't behave correctly just gets taken away. It's not right. I'm sure it isn't."

Now Rebecca knew why she'd felt uneasy, uncomfortable with some of the things Mark had told her. Yes, Zanu had created a peaceful world, but at what price?

"You're right," she said to Tara, "peace shouldn't mean that you have to give up being free. It shouldn't! But where do they take the people they arrest? Do you have any idea? And why did they take your parents?"

"My parents started asking questions about Laura and now about Jonathon. They couldn't just sit by and let them disappear like that! They knew I might be left alone if they questioned the authorities. But I wouldn't let that stop them. I couldn't, it wouldn't have been right." Tara paused. "I don't know where Zanu takes them. Jonathon always thought it was up north somewhere, where it's cold and snowy, or to such an isolated, lonely place that no guards or police would be needed. And of course, even if someone did escape and make it back to civilization they'd be picked up again the second they set foot in the city."

"Why would they get caught so easily?"

"There's a force field around the city. All travel is strictly controlled by Zanu."

Rebecca began to realize how powerful Zanu really was, and that she was in a very precarious situation.

"Look, Tara," she said, "if what you say about Zanu is true, I'd better get back to Mark's. If they're watching everything, they might know I'm not there. And," she added, "I want to help you, but I also want to get back to my home and to my time. In fact, maybe there's something I can do! Maybe I could tell the police chief that I won't go home unless he frees your family. He *knows* he has to send me back—he said something about not messing up this present. Anyway, we'll think of something!"

She squeezed Tara's hand in encouragement. They walked to the front of the house. Tara was just about to go in when Rebecca grabbed her arm.

"Look," Rebecca whispered, "There's a skimmer in front of Mark's house! Oh no, they're not after him too! Wait here, I'm going to try to get closer and see if I can hear them."

Rebecca ran from tree to tree, grateful for the complete blackness which surrounded her. Finally she scurried under a large fir just beside Mark's house.

The police guards were talking to Mark in his doorway.

"We picked up a communication," one of them said, "from Kobrin's, twenty minutes ago. We were sure she would be back here by now. She must be found and brought to the police centre. The chief told me personally that when they checked her file it read that she mysteriously disappeared on July 3, 1986. She was never seen or heard from again. It was assumed that she was kidnapped and murdered. We cannot let her return to 1986 now because somehow that could change our present. She must be found. If she turns up, call us immediately. We will search Kobrin's house and grounds. The Kobrin girl

will also have to be taken in." And they turned to the police
vehicle.

Rebecca, her heart pounding so hard she was sure they
could hear it, turned and scrambled back to the place
where Tara was still waiting. She reached her just before
the police skimmer pulled up to the Kobrin's house.

"C'mon," she said, grabbing Tara's hand, pulling her
toward the lane. "They're after us both!"

CHAPTER SIX
The Chase

"Quick," said Tara, "my skimmer."

They ran as fast as they could to the back lane and climbed into the skimmer. Tara pushed some controls, the skimmer lifted off and they drove down the back lane with their lights out.

"Where can we go?" asked Rebecca. "Is there anywhere we can hide?"

"I don't know, I can't think!" cried Tara. "I don't know anyone who could hide us . . ."

She was driving very fast. Up and down lanes.

"Well, let's get out of the city then. We can hide in the country 'til we figure out something."

"No, there's a force field. We can't get out."

"There must be somewhere we can go!"

Tara was crying.

"There isn't. There isn't. They'll catch us. They have radar. They have all kinds of machines. They'll track us down in no time."

"What about friends, you must have friends who would help hide you."

"Hide us from Zanu?" wailed Tara. "We'd just get my friends in trouble."

"Tara!" screamed Rebecca. "Pull yourself together! Think!"

Tara took some deep, gulping breaths. The skimmer continued to speed up and down dark lanes.

In the momentary silence Rebecca could feel her heart pounding. Her hands had turned to ice. The realization had struck her—she was in the worst danger she could possibly be in. Presumed dead. Murdered. Never returned. The words echoed in her head. If Zanu captured her they'd never return her to her own time. And, she realized, thinking further than she wanted to, they would probably kill her to make sure she could never escape back. Chills shot up and down her spine as this thought sank in. Never see her family and friends again. Murdered—and not even in her own time. She realized that her teeth were chattering, and her whole body was shaking. Tara continued to let out big gulping sobs.

"Stop it!" Rebecca said, as firmly as she could through her chattering teeth. "This has to stop. We have to be calm. If they catch us, we have to be ready, alert. A chance may come to escape. At any point. We have to be ready to take it. If we're hysterical wrecks we've already given up."

Tara looked at her. Rebecca's firmness and conviction startled her into silence. She took a deep breath.

"I'm sorry," she snivelled, "you're right, of course. I'll try. I'll try." She paused. "Maybe there is someone . . . "

"Who? Who?" urged Rebecca.

"Someone Jonathon mentioned, then Mother."

"Who? Where are they?"

"They live near the outskirts of the city," said Tara. "4430—

564 Street. Mother made me memorize it. But if we get them in trouble?"

"We won't drive up to their front door!" exclaimed Rebecca. "We'll park the skimmer a little way from the house—we'll sneak up."

"Oh! Look!" cried Tara. "A guard skim." Up ahead, passing along a cross street, a pair of lights flashed and was gone.

Tara backed her skimmer up and programmed the computer to take them at top speed to the outskirts of town. It only took a few minutes to get there. Tara drove past the house. Then they drove to the end of the block and stopped the skimmer.

Suddenly, seemingly out of nowhere, lights appeared in front of them, then behind them. The lights drew closer and closer, then stopped, blocking the girls' way. It was two guard skimmers.

"Oh, no," moaned Rebecca.

Tara brought the skimmer to a stop.

"Isn't there any way out?" Rebecca cried, "Make a break for it, Tara. Drive through them! They'll kill us anyway!" But Tara seemed frozen by fear and didn't respond.

Two guards leapt out of the first skimmer and stood on either side of their skimmer. Two more from the rear skimmer joined them. Lasers were pointed at their heads. The guards motioned them to get out.

As Tara's hand reached for the release button on the computer dash, to open her door, a flash of light zapped across the blackness and the two guards on her side slumped to the ground. Rebecca watched in total astonishment as the same thing happened on her side. Within seconds a young woman and a young man, one on Rebecca's side of the skimmer, the other on Tara's, were tapping on their windows. They were dressed all in black, even their faces blackened over. Tara stared at the one by her window but didn't move.

"Tara!" hissed Rebeca. "Roll down the windows! These people want to talk to us!"

As if she were a robot obeying orders, Tara pressed the window control.

"You must leave the city," the young woman on Tara's side said in a whisper as soon as the window was open. "In exactly ten minutes there will be a force field open at these co-ordinates." She handed Tara a slip of paper. "Feed that into your computer. Be there."

The young man then handed Rebecca a small black triangular object. "This is a jamming device." He pressed a small button. The device glowed a faint red. "It is now activated. It will jam all frequencies. Once you are clear of the city you must try to find others who have been cut loose. It's your only hope. This is all we can do. Now go!"

"Good luck," whispered the young woman, and they both disappeared into the night.

Tara sat immobilized.

"Tara," said Rebecca, reaching over and shaking her. "Feed that into your computer. Now! We have ten minutes. Get us out of here!"

"But," Tara was still in a daze. "Who . . . why . . . ?"

"Never mind that! Can you feed the directions into your computer?"

Tara looked at the piece of paper for a moment—which seemed like an eternity to Rebecca—then nodded. The dash computer was lit up so that one could easily program it, even at night. Tara, her hands shaking so much she could barely push the right numbers, fed the information into the computer.

"It's done," she said.

"Then let's go!" Rebecca commanded.

Tara nodded again. She raised the skimmer above the level of the other two, and they sped away.

"Who on earth were those people?" asked Rebecca. "They appeared right out of nowhere . . . "

"And how did they know we needed help?" added Tara, her voice still very weak.

"Yes, how?" mused Rebecca. "The only other person who knew about me being with you was . . . Mark. That policeman told Mark." She paused and looked at Tara. "Mark? No, he would have helped Zanu catch us, I think. Or . . . "

It was too confusing. She couldn't think straight. And she knew they weren't out of danger. Even if by some miracle they did get out of the city, how would they find other people who could help them? And how, how, could she *ever* get back to that time machine and home again?

"We're approaching the force field," announced Tara. The skimmer drew up in front of a faint shimmering white glow which seemed to extend as far as the eye could see both to the right and the left as well as from the ground up. They could see nothing through it. They waited then, both thinking but afraid to say it, that they might be too late. Then suddenly, right in front of them, a black hole seemed to grow, pushing aside the light.

Tara, again, seemed to freeze.

"Go! Go!" Rebecca urged. "Tara!"

Tara looked at Rebecca. "Maybe it's better to be captured. We'll be all alone out there. I'm scared."

"Tara," pleaded Rebecca, "I'm scared, too. But it's our only chance. Our only *real* chance. Being caught is no chance at all."

Tara pondered this for a moment, then she pushed the button. This time Rebecca watched what she did. The thought had occurred to her that she might have to take over at some point if Tara collapsed. The skimmer moved forward through the black hole.

Rebecca could feel a pull on the skimmer, it shuddered as it pushed against an invisible force. She shuddered too, wondering if the skimmer would disintegrate under the stress of the force field, and if she and Tara would be destroyed along with it. But in the next instant the skimmer bolted like a horse set free and shot away from the force field into an all-encompassing blackness.

CHAPTER SEVEN
The Void

It was black. A blackness so complete it was overwhelming. It was the stuff nightmares are made of, small children's fears, an almost nothingness. There were no stars, no moon, no haze from city or town lights. The little light beams the skimmer emitted seemed to be swallowed up the moment they left their source.

Tara raised the skimmer to its highest level in order to avoid any trees which might be there, and they flew like a low-flying craft over the land.

Rebecca had never experienced such emptiness, such blackness. Both she and Tara were quiet now, staring into the awesome space around them. Rebecca felt lost, completely and totally lost. Where were they going? North? What would they find? Other people? Could you live out there? Was it dangerous? Were there bears, or wolves? Could they make a fire? Would they survive? She was frightened. Very frightened. She'd been in some tight spots before, but never had she felt so alone.

She wasn't alone though. She looked at Tara. How would Tara manage out here? Perhaps she would just give up and die. Tara's eyes were closed and she seemed to be half asleep. It was so quiet. The skimmer hummed on, a gentle vibration lulling them both . . . Rebecca's eyes began to close, despite her effort to watch for something—anything—any break in the dark.

Rebecca sat up with a jolt. The sun was streaming into the skimmer. Tara was still fast asleep beside her.

Rebecca looked at her watch. It was 4:30 A.M. She felt groggy, disoriented. How could they have fallen asleep? Perhaps it was the shock. Sleep protected their minds from taking in too much, from going crazy. She squinted at Tara. She was still sleeping. Rebecca looked around and down. They were flying over a small lake surrounded by forest. The conifers were a peculiar colour for midsummer—brown on the tops and on one side. Must be the windward side, Rebecca thought. But what had caused them to turn brown? The leaves of the other trees—birches, and oaks mainly—also had a yellowish brown hue, not the rich green she so loved at this time of year. There was no sign of life anywhere.

Should she let Tara sleep or should she wake her? A moment later the decision was made for her.

"Tara! Tara! Wake up! I see something! No, I see somebody. I mean some bodies. I see some people!"

Tara opened her eyes and sat bolt upright. A look of terror swept over her face.

"Oh, I'm sorry I frightened you Tara, it's just, we just passed over some people." Rebecca turned her head to look through the back window, hoping to pick out some landmarks to help remember where she had spotted those people.

Tara looked at Rebecca and then looked around. She

seemed bewildered. "But where are we? What is all that?"
She pointed below them.

"Well, I don't know where we are," Rebecca answered,
still craned around, looking back. "But I saw some people. Turn this thing around so we can find them again.
If we go much farther we'll lose them."

"But," objected Tara, "we don't know who they are. If
they were cut loose they could be criminals, or . . . or . . . "

"Tara! Come on! You were cut loose, and your parents
and Jonathon and your sister—and you're hardly criminals.
Who knows—it may be some of your family down there!"

Tara turned the skimmer around and headed back the
way they'd come. The people were grouped just at the far
end of the lake. They were huddled together, sleeping
under the trees. Just beside them, right at the water's edge,
there was a natural clearing. Tara set the skimmer down.
By the time they were on the ground all the people had
awakened and were sitting up, watching the girls' skimmer. Tara leaned forward, frowning, as she looked through
the windshield, then shook her head.

"No one I know," she sighed.

It was a small group—six people. There were two elderly
people, a man and a woman, two women who looked as
if they would be in their twenties, a tall, lanky boy
somewhere in his teens and a very young boy.

"Look at that little boy!" exclaimed Rebecca. "What could
he possibly have done to end up here!"

They all looked drawn and pale, their cheeks sunken,
their eyes dull. Their once-beautiful clothes were only tat-
ters now, which they somehow gathered around themselves.

The tall, lanky boy stepped forward. His legs seemed
to give way beneath him for a moment but with obvious

effort he pulled himself up straight and walked towards the skimmer.

"C'mon," said Rebecca, "open the doors. I want to talk to them."

Tara, with obvious reluctance, pressed the button and the doors opened. Rebecca climbed out. Her bones cracked and she realized her neck and back hurt from sleeping upright for hours. The early morning chill bit through her thin clothes, and she shivered. She managed a tentative smile as she approached the young man and said "Hi!"

"Hello," he responded, with a smile that was quite dazzling in its openness and warmth. Now that she saw him closer she thought he looked about 15 or 16 years old. He had large brown eyes in a long face, and long, straight brown hair which was tangled and looked like it hadn't been washed for weeks.

"Dare I ask," he continued, "how on earth you got here?"

"In this, of course," replied Rebecca, turning towards the skimmer.

Tara got out of the skimmer and came around to stand beside Rebecca. The cool air seemed to shock her and she wrapped her arms around herself. She began to shiver.

"Yes," he said, "I can see that, but how on earth did you get out in a skimmer? And who are you? You seem too young to be Zanu guards."

Rebecca grimaced. "We're not Zanu guards," she said with disgust. "We're being chased by them, in fact. We got into this skimmer and tried to escape, but they caught us, and then suddenly we were rescued by some strangers. They told us how to escape the force field—and here we are."

The young man nodded. He looked very solemn. "That's good, very good. It means they're getting organized, well organized—you won't be the last they'll help.

"Who," asked Rebecca, "who were they?"

"Oh," he laughed, "I don't know their names, but I do know that there's a group of people who are working together against Zanu. They want to return the world to democracy. A true democracy."

"Oh," breathed Rebecca, "like an underground movement."

"Yes," he said, "that's what it is."

"Excuse me," Tara interrupted, "but what are you doing here?"

The young man looked at her. "Well," he said, a faint smile on his face, "I believe we're dying."

Tara blanched.

"I'm sorry to alarm you," he said, "I'd like to put a better light on it—and now that you've arrived there might be hope. He stopped and his face seemed to brighten, "Maybe we could use the skimmer somehow . . . "

While he was talking, the others had begun to gather round the skimmer.

The small boy walked up to Tara and Rebecca. He was thin, with blond curly hair, blue eyes and pale skin, which was blistered and red from the sun.

"What's your names?" the boy asked, looking up at Tara and Rebecca, grabbing the bottom of Tara's shirt in his little fist.

Tara managed a smile and crouched down to his level. "My name is Tara," she replied, "and this is my friend Rebecca. What's your name?"

"Paul," he said, "and I'm *very* bad."

"Are you, Paul?" asked Tara.

"Oh, yes!" declared Paul. "I don't like to buy new toys, I like my old ones. I won't throw them in the disinamator, I won't! And I won't go shopping with Mommy and Daddy. I lie on the ground and scream and scream. And," he said, his eyes growing very wide, "I smashed our computer into bits."

Rebecca listened in amazement.

"And they sent you here, because of *that*?"

Paul nodded and tried to look brave.

"Where are your Mommy and Daddy?" asked Tara.

"At home," the boy whispered, as he fought back tears.

Tara put her arms around him and hugged him. Paul started to pull away, but then climbed into her lap and wrapped his arms around her neck.

They were very near the shore of the lake, the trees just a few metres behind them. They were standing on a dull, brown gravel surface, which changed to sand nearer the water. The few scraggly bushes growing just behind the gravel were stunted and yellowish. The forest also looked thinned out, sparse.

"Ouch!" yelped Tara, swatting her neck.

"What is it? What's the matter?" asked Rebecca.

"I don't know, my neck, it hurts. Ouch!" she exclaimed again.

Suddenly Rebecca slapped her cheek and inspected her hand.

"Oh, Tara," she moaned, "it's mosquitoes, and probably black flies if it really hurts."

"And horseflies, wasps, all sorts of mean creatures," laughed the young man. He had a wonderful, infectious laugh. "We're probably the first food they've had in a long time. Most of the animals seem to be gone. Oh," he said, "excuse me, please meet the others." He held out his arm toward the elderly couple. "This is Sonya and David." Then he indicated the two young women, "Kristin and Rachel, and you've met Paul."

"And you?" asked Rebecca.

"Oh, I'm Michael."

"Don't you have any shelter here?" asked Rebecca, looking around.

"No shelter," replied Michael blithely, "no food, and the water is undrinkable."

"You can't drink the water?" Rebecca said with dismay. "Why not?" Suddenly she felt terribly hungry and terribly thirsty.

"It's polluted," said David, his voice flat and bitter. "It's dead and rotten, like everything around us. A wasteland."

"But," objected Rebecca, "it's not possible! Why, I've travelled up north, it's beautiful, it's not dead. There are tons of animals. The water has algae in it, but I mean, you just boil it and . . . "

Rebecca realized they were all looking at her very strangely.

"You'd better explain," suggested Tara, "they don't know what you're talking about."

"Well," said Rebecca, "I'm from 1986."

"What?" laughed Michael. "That's a good joke."

"It's no joke," Rebecca said patiently. "I wish it was. Do you want to hear the whole story?"

"Absolutely," stated Michael, and he got everyone to sit down around Rebecca. As briefly as she could, she told them of her journey from another time.

"It's hard to believe you're from our past," Michael said, when she'd finished. "There are so many questions I'd like to ask you."

"Yes, well, there's some questions I'd like to ask you," said Rebecca. "Why did those people send us out of the city? There's nothing out here. Nothing. Why couldn't they have helped us hide in the city? And," she paused and looked around, "*why* is there nothing out here? I don't understand. Why is it a wasteland? It used to be so beautiful. You could fish, swim, drink the water—as long as it was boiled. What happened?"

"I told you," replied David, "pollution. When the big corporations took over, they cared more about making money than about anything else. They got around the pollution controls, they polluted the air and the water—and now you can see the result."

"And as to your first question," Michael interrupted, "we can only guess why they sent you out here. Before I was cut loose there was talk of setting up a network in the north, a base we could work from and a place to send people who were cut loose. They must've hoped that you'd find some people, like us, and we'd use the skimmer. They may also have been afraid you'd be caught in the city. And we can, we *can* use this skimmer. This could be just the chance we've been waiting for."

"But how can you set up anything here?" asked Rebecca. "If it's truly a wasteland, no one can survive here. What do you eat and drink?" She paused and looked at the group. "How long have you been here?"

"Five days," answered Michael, "this is our sixth. They gave us enough water to last six days. Enough food pills to last three days."

Rebecca looked at him in disbelief. "But why . . . I don't understand . . . why not just shoot you? I mean, why the charade? Water for a week . . . ?" She looked around at the gaunt faces. "It's a slow death. It's torture!"

"I'm afraid you've answered your own question," David replied.

"No," she shook her head, "I can't believe it. Why would they want to torture people? What would they get out of it?"

"We may learn the answer to that question any time now," answered David, his voice grim.

"Yes," Rachel spoke for the first time, "they said they'd return in six days."

"Then we'd better get away, fast!" cried Tara, jumping up and grabbing Rebecca's sleeve.

"No. No, wait!" Michael said. "You can't go. Not now. We can hide you in the forest until they're gone. If they kill us, at least you'll know what happens out here. You can warn others perhaps."

"What's the use of that?" cried Tara. "Why warn them? Where can they go? No food, no shelter, no water purifiers anywhere . . ."

"I don't know," Michael persisted, "but perhaps we can discover something about their reasons, their plans. Stay. Please. I think there's a slim chance we can put you and your skimmer to some use. I just need some time to think . . ."

"Michael," interrupted Rachel, "shouldn't we get them hidden if they're going to stay?"

"Yes, of course." He looked at Rebecca and Tara. Tara was still clutching Rebecca's sleeve, poised to run.

"Will you stay?"

"I think we should, Tara," said Rebecca. "We'll be no good out there in the wilderness on our own. Michael's right. Here, with the skimmer we might be of use."

Tara dropped Rebecca's sleeve. "I suppose you're right," she said, reluctantly.

"Come on then," said Michael, "We'll move you into the forest, out of sight. Keep your jamming device on so their radar can't see you. And we'll have to cover the skimmer somehow so their own eyes won't catch you. May I drive?" he asked Tara politely.

"Yes," she replied, smiling in spite of her anxiety, at his kind and pleasant tone.

"I'm getting to know the woods quite well," he remarked,

climbing into the skimmer. "I think I can manoeuver it into a large clump of bush about half a kilometre in."

Rebecca, Tara and Paul got into the skimmer with him, Tara in front so she could show him her personal code, Rebecca and Paul in the rear.

Michael started the skimmer, and eased it into the forest, curving in and around trees and bushes, keeping it slightly above the ground and rock of the forest floor.

Eventually he came to a stop by a large clump of bushes.

Rebecca, Tara and Paul climbed out and looked around. Rebecca studied the bushes. They were about three metres high, and the branches were slender. They could probably be bent, she thought.

"If we can somehow make a hole, that skimmer could just sit inside there." She was thinking out loud and hadn't noticed that Tara wasn't beside her.

"Tara?"

Tara was leaning against a tree. Her face was ashen, and she was breathing in shallow gasps.

"What is it, Tara? You look sick."

"I feel . . . I don't know. There's so much sky. So many trees. And the trees are so ugly. These things are biting me. The air feels sticky. It's getting too hot. I feel dizzy. It's . . . I hate it out here! I want to go home! Oh, I want to go home!" And she sank down onto the ground, sobbing.

"Don't cry! Don't cry!" Paul said, tugging Tara's top. "Don't be sad!"

Rebecca put her arms around Tara. "You will go home, Tara. You will." Suddenly Rebecca felt like crying, too. She knew how Tara felt. She wanted to go home, too.

Michael was out of the skimmer, kneeling beside them.

"We all want to go home, Tara," he said gently. "And we

will. Someday. But first, we have lots of work to do." He looked at the bushes.

"I'm going to try to force a hole into that bush by moving the skimmer forward very slowly."

He got back into the skimmer and began to nudge the bushes. Some simply cracked and broke, while others bent as if they had little life left in them. Once the skimmer was well within the bush, they all worked together to cover it. Tears flowed down Tara's cheeks as she snapped branches off the trees and threw them over the skimmer. Rebecca was astounded at how brittle and fragile the branches were. It was terrifying to think of an entire world slowly dying.

She thought of the beauty and the strength of the trees from her time—but even then . . . when they had driven to Falcon Lake last year she'd noticed huge stretches of brown, dying leaves on the windward side of the forest. Her mouth felt dry. She was scared. Was her world dying around her and she hadn't realized it?

CHAPTER EIGHT
The Wait

"You'd better get back into the skimmer," Michael said to Rebecca and Tara. "We don't want their radar picking up two unidentified bodies. I'll be back as soon as I know something." He paused. "If I'm not back by nightfall you'd best come and have a look. Come on, Paul. And Paul, not a word to the guards about our new friends, all right? This will just be our little secret."

Paul nodded his head earnestly, took Michael's hand and they walked away into the forest, back the way they'd come.

"C'mon," said Rebecca to Tara, "let's get in. They could arrive any time." The girls bent the bushes back and squeezed into the skimmer. They sank back into the plush seat. Just then they heard, through the unnatural quiet of the forest, a distinctly man-made sound. It was a low hum. They could see nothing, however, through their cover.

"Must be an air machine," said Tara.

"Do you think they can see us from the air?" she added, brushing away tears, wiping her nose with her sleeve.

"I hope not," answered Rebecca, her voice curt. She felt sorry for Tara, but suddenly, she felt irritated as well.

Sometimes she can be a real wimp, Rebecca thought, feeling very cross. Aloud she said, "You know Tara, those people camped by the lake could be being—well, I don't know—tortured or shot—at this very moment. As we sit here talking. *We're* safe. They aren't." Actually, Rebecca didn't feel very safe at all. But she felt they should at least try to be brave.

Tara looked at Rebecca. She was surprised by Rebecca's sharp tone.

"We're hardly what I would call safe, Rebecca. We have no food, no water, nowhere to go . . . "

"Oh, stop it, Tara!" Rebecca almost screamed. "Just stop it! I'm well aware of that. You don't have to keep saying it over and over . . . "

They both fell silent then. The silence stretched out and out and out. Rebecca began to feel badly. After all, how would she feel, she thought to herself, if she were left completely alone—her whole family gone—maybe dead—still—Tara could try to *do* something—sitting around feeling sorry for herself . . .

"You're right, Rebecca."

"What?" Rebecca was startled. She wondered if she had been muttering her thoughts aloud without realizing it.

"I've been so worried about getting caught and what they could do to me, I haven't even given a thought to anyone else. I mean, maybe Michael is right—maybe we can use the skimmer . . . Oh!" she exclaimed, for Michael was staring into the window.

Tara opened the window.

"What is it?" she asked, her voice trembling.

"They've come and gone," said Michael, looking quite grim. "But they'll be back. Come out of there. We have to talk."

The girls scrambled out of the skimmer and out of the bushes they'd covered it with. Michael sat down and leaned against a tree. Rebecca could see that he was exhausted and weak from so much walking. He held out a small flask. "Water. They left us some." He handed it to Tara. She gulped it down.

"Go easy," he cautioned. "You may need some later."

Tara blushed and passed the flask to Rebecca. She took three large gulps, then made herself stop and offered the flask to Michael. She had never realized how wonderful cool water could be. It was the best taste in the world.

He shook his head. "You keep it. If you agree with my plan, I won't need it."

"What happened?" asked Rebecca, clutching the flask.

"They're keeping us alive for a very good reason," said Michael. "Information."

"Information?" asked Tara.

"You mean," asked Rebecca, "information as in, informers?"

Michael looked into her eyes, appreciating her quickness. "Right," he nodded. "We supply them with names of people in the city who are possible malcontents, they rescue us. They take us to the Zanu headquarters on an island not far from here, feed us, care for us, then let us live in a supervised camp. Well taken care of."

"That's awful," murmured Rebecca. "It would be so hard to refuse them."

"Harder and harder," Michael agreed, "as the days go by and you know you'll die if you refuse—and you get sick from drinking the water and need medical attention. Oh yes, they're clever."

"What's your plan?" asked Rebecca.

"I'll tell them I'm ready to give names. I'll go with them. Then I'll be in the compound. All the food and supplies we need are there. If I can locate them, maybe you and your skimmer can get close enough so that I can get some out—and then we can really set up a hideout."

Now it was Rebecca's turn to be scared.

"You know, Michael," she said, her voice a little high and thin, "if they catch me, they'll kill me."

"I know, Rebecca, and I don't want that to happen—not only because I don't want you hurt, but because somehow we have to get you back to your time alive. You see, I've been thinking that if we can do that, this present might never happen. After all, from what you say, according to Zanu records, you never returned to 1986."

"That's true," Rebecca agreed.

"So maybe just sending you back would be enough to change our present."

"Well," agreed Rebecca, "that's what that police guard seemed to think. That's why they don't want to send me back."

"So, we have to get you back. And," he continued, "letting you starve to death out here is not going to get you back. My plan may be dangerous but don't you see, it's no more hazardous than sitting here dying a slow death. It may just be quicker there, that's all. At least let's go and face it! And it just might work."

Rebeca looked at him. He was quite right. She couldn't argue with his logic.

Suddenly Tara spoke up.

"I want to go, too. I'm not going to just sit here all alone and die of starvation!"

"Of course you have to go," smiled Michael. "Who else would drive the skimmer?"

Tara responded with a wan smile. "That's true," she said, "isn't it?"

"They'll be back shortly," said Michael, "to see which of us has broken. We've all decided that both Rachel and I should go. The others are too weak to do anything once they got there. Now, I have no idea how this place is set up, how heavily guarded it is—anything. You'll have to try to land as close as possible without being detected. Rachel and I will keep our eyes and ears open. If we can, we'll steal the goods before you arrive. If we can't, I hope we can at least find out where they're stored. Perhaps the place won't be too heavily guarded—against what, after all? Their radar could detect anything. An army of weaponless, starving people swimming the lake to their island is unlikely, and no threat anyway."

"When should we come?" asked Rebecca.

"Tonight," replied Michael. "After midnight. We'll try to leave a sign, or watch for you, or something. If we can.

"Tara, I'll program your skimmer computer with the correct co-ordinates to get you there. We passed it on the way here so I have a pretty good idea of where it is."

Michael forced himself up and went to program the computer. Rebecca and Tara looked into each other's eyes.

"At least it's a chance, Tara," Rebecca said.

"I know," Tara agreed as she swatted a mosquito on her leg and then lowered her eyes to the ground to make sure no other strange insect was about to crawl on her. "I just wish I were home."

So do I, thought Rebecca, so do I.

After a few moments Michael emerged from the skimmer.

"I have to get back," he said. He took their hands. "Good luck," he smiled. "Don't look so gloomy. We'll be in and out of there in no time!" He gave their hands a squeeze, winked, and hurried off.

Rebecca and Tara looked at each other. Rebecca wiped her forehead. It was only 9 o'clock in the morning, but it was already very hot. A black fly buzzed around her head.

"Let's wait in the skimmer," she suggested. "At least the bugs won't eat us up."

Tara nodded and they climbed into the skimmer to wait the interminable wait, until nightfall.

CHAPTER NINE

Waiting for The Night to Come

Rebecca and Tara listened to the sound of the air machine. They heard it arrive, then leave again.

It was stifling hot in their small skimmer.

"Doesn't this thing have an air conditioner?" Rebecca asked, her voice irritable and whiny.

"A what?"

"An air conditioner! You know. A cooling machine—to make the air cooler. You'd think in this day and age they'd all have them—standard equipment."

"What for? The air in the city never gets hot. *It* is temperature-controlled, so our houses and skimmers don't need such things."

"Oh, right, of course," sighed Rebecca. "Well, I don't want to sit here all day, do you?"

Rebecca, who could ususally sit for hours reading a good book, or watching a good movie, now found her legs almost twitching to move. She felt restless and anxious.

She tried not to think about the night to come, but it was almost impossible not to.

"Let's go talk to the others while we wait," she said finally. "At least we can try to keep our minds busy. And," she added, "I've got lots of questions I want answered."

They found the small group resting under the shade of some birch trees. Paul was sleeping, his head on Sonya's lap. She also had her eyes closed and seemed to be asleep. David and Kristen were staring into the distance.

"Oh, hello!" they said when they saw the girls approaching.

"Hi!" said Rebecca. "May we sit with you awhile?"

David looked gravely at Rebecca. "Of course, my dear," he said. "Sit down. It's not often we get to talk to someone from our very own past."

"Oh, yes," said Kristen, as the girls settled themselves into the meagre shade of the birch trees. "Please tell us what it was like back then. It sounds like it was a terribly dangerous world."

Rebecca couldn't keep herself from snorting, "Not like yours, you mean?"

Kristen smiled back. She was a tall young woman with long black hair and large grey eyes. "I suppose," she sighed, "the world has always been a rather dangerous place."

"I guess it has," Rebecca agreed. "I'm in a group that is working to get the world to disarm—to be nuclear free. And there's poverty in the world—in Winnipeg, too. But there is a good side—I can say what I want and when I'm 18 I can vote, and I go to school, I don't have to work."

"You know," David said, "big business already ran much of your so-called democracy even then. You were just unaware of it."

"What do you mean?" asked Rebecca.

"I mean," said David, "it was big business and all their

money who really had t[...]
back to just that time. Ev[...]
how Zanu began. Because t[...]
government couldn't really st[...]
they pleased, and in fact, the so-[...]
ally supported and defended, even[...]
corporations. So they got away with p[...]
ment." He gestured around them. "And, [...] here
was the arms race, of course. That was v[...] usiness
and pollution from nuclear accidents is still v[...] much with
us."

"I find it hard to believe," Rebecca objected, "that pollution could change things *so* much."

"Oh, yes," said David. "First there was acid rain. It killed the lakes and is killing the trees, so the animals have died from starvation. Then there was 'the greenhouse effect'."

"Yes, we've studied that in school," said Rebecca. "Too much carbon dioxide in the atmosphere could make a sort of blanket of gas around the earth, the sun could get in but the heat couldn't get out, so the temperature of the earth would rise."

"That's correct," David nodded. "Carbon dioxide, chlorofluoro carbons, methane, nitrous oxide. These substances accumulated in the atmosphere and trapped heat—what we called 'the greenhouse effect'. It developed rapidly once they started cutting down the South American rainforests. Without the trees to utilize the carbon dioxide it just stayed in the atmosphere—in huge quantities. The prairies are now a dust bowl, the lakes are evaporating—or being drained for water, which we then purify. The North is, from what I can see, a dead place. The Polar and glacial ice has been melting, and that has produced huge floods. New York is all under water now."

Rebecca sank back against the tree.

your world seemed like such a good
ease, no wars, lots of gorgeous clothes and
everybody . . . "

I remember voting in the last election before Zanu took control," said David wistfully. "I was thirty then. Working as a computer programmer. I liked my job, except that I had to go where they told me to go, train where they wanted me to train, do what they wanted me to do. But I had no choice—I had to live, to eat, after all. With the unemployment that started in the 70s we had to hang onto our jobs. No one dared complain. They were glad to be working. Governments were being "realistic" and "responsible," trying to reduce deficits and cutting back on aid to the poor. You had to work to live. What choice did we have?" He shook his head.

"There are always choices." Rebecca turned to see who was contradicting David. It was the old woman, Sonya. "We could have fought them. We could have been more concerned while we had the chance to change things. It would have been better than this—and perhaps this never would have happened. But never mind," she said, smiling at Rebecca, "we'll get you back alive. I'm sure of it—and then—maybe we'll get another chance—somehow."

"A fan," said Rebecca, "a fan."

"What?" asked David.

But his voice began to sound far away. It was hot, so hot. Kristen was asking Tara about her family. Rebecca's eyes grew heavy. The air shimmered around her. She lay down on the ground and closed her eyes, listening to Tara talk about her sister and brother. And before she knew it, she was asleep.

When she woke it was still light. Her throat was so parched she couldn't swallow. She sat up. Everyone around her was asleep, sprawled out on the ground under the trees, except Paul, who was splashing in the water of the lake. She looked at him dreamily. It looked so wonderful, so cool. Maybe she'd join him. She reached over and took a small sip of the water in her flask. That was better. At least she could swallow now, and then the thought hit her.

"Paul!" she screamed, leaping up, "Paul, come out of there! Paul!" She felt herself running, running. But it was too late. When she got to the edge of the lake she could see him ducking under, swallowing water, splashing. "Oh, Paul!" she cried, "come out. That water's bad. You mustn't swallow it. Come out, please!"

"No!" he yelled. "Don't want to. Want to watch me swim?" He dogpaddled a bit. "My mommy taught me!"

"Paul!" Rebecca commanded, putting on her sternest babysitter voice. "You come out this minute or you'll be in big trouble."

Paul looked at her doubtfully for a moment, then smiled. "I don't care," he said, "I'm always in big trouble."

Tara was standing beside Rebecca now. The others were all awake, watching.

"Paul," she said softly.

He looked at her.

"Want to come in, Tara?"

"No, Paul, I can't," she answered. "But Paul, come here for a minute. I have to tell you something."

Reluctantly Paul splashed to the sandy edge of the lake. "What?" he asked suspiciously.

"You know," she said, "Rebecca and I have to go away tonight. And when we come back, there's one thing I'd like better than anything in the whole world."

"What?" Paul asked, his suspicion giving way to curiosity.

"A little brother."

"Really?" asked Paul, looking up into Tara's eyes. Then he was distracted by a horsefly which started to circle around and around his head. He tried to hit it, but couldn't. Finally it flew off to bother Rebecca.

"Yes," Tara answered, when she had his attention again, "really. All my family is gone, just like yours, and well, I thought maybe we could be a family, just you and I."

He looked at her seriously for a moment, considering her words.

"All right," he answered finally.

"Good," sighed Tara in relief.

Paul turned and splashed back into the water up to his waist.

"No, wait," she called to him, "don't go back in there. If you're to be my family you have to stay healthy. And you might get sick if you swim in that water. So come out now. I want a good, strong, healthy brother."

Paul turned back and looked at Tara. He looked at the water. He smacked the water with the palm of his hand and watched until the concentric circles he had produced had faded away. He sighed, then he walked out, digging his feet into the sandy bottom of the lake to slow his progress as much as possible. Tara bent down and picked him up. He wrapped his arms around her.

Rebecca, Paul and Tara walked back under the trees. They talked and waited, until finally the sun began to set.

"I think it's time," Rebecca said. "We should get back to the skimmer while there's still some light."

Paul threw his arms around Tara and clung to her. Rebecca could see his little body shivering.

"He's burning," Tara said to Rebecca, holding him close.

"My tummy hurts," Paul complained.

"Don't worry, Paul," Tara whispered in his ear. "We'll

bring food and water and some medicine to make your tummy better."

"I *hate* medicine!"

Tara laughed. "I know, I hate it too."

"Now be a good boy," Rebecca said in a stern voice. "No more swimming in the lake. O.K.?" And she ruffled his hair with her hand.

Kristen had to pull Paul off Tara's neck. Rebecca and Tara said goodbye to the others, then turned and hurried into the forest. It was still very hot and the mosquitoes were terrible. Tara, in her short pants and sleeveless top, was covered in bites and getting more every minute. They were even biting Rebecca through her thin silk clothes. Rebecca and Tara ran scrambling over dead branches, their boots sinking slightly into a layer of dead, reddish-brown pine needles which carpeted the forest floor. Soon they were at the skimmer. They leapt in, shutting out most of the bugs. Tara manoeuvred the skimmer out of the bush and into a small clearing.

Again they had to wait. They occupied their time by killing all the mosquitoes in the skimmer. Finally, the sun set. Clouds scudded across the sky, a full moon peaked through when it could.

Rebecca looked at her watch. 11:45 P.M.

"Let's go," she said to Tara.

Tara started the skimmer. It lifted straight up out of the trees. Then she instructed the computer to follow the co-ordinates Michael had fed into it earlier that day. The skimmer turned slightly, then raced over the trees. They were on their way to Zanu headquarters.

CHAPTER TEN
Zanu Headquarters

"This is crazy," muttered Rebecca. "We don't know where they are, or how to find them or, or, anything!" Her teeth were chattering and her whole body shook.

"We know they're on an island and we have to land away from the complex," said Tara, sounding almost calm.

Rebecca looked at her in surprise.

"Aren't you scared?" she said, her teeth chattering so violently she could barely get the words out.

Tara managed a weak smile. "Yes," she said, "I'm terrified. But . . . I don't know . . . seeing Paul so helpless there, and thinking about my family and about what Sonya said—well, we have a real chance to help now. And I'm going to try my best and," she murmured, "maybe they have medicine there. Paul is going to need medicine. I don't think his body is strong enough to fight alone."

Rebecca nodded. She took a deep breath. She tried to stop herself from shaking. If Tara could pull herself together like that, then so could she.

A strong wind was picking up and the small skimmer began to shake. It tilted to one side, straightening out with a bump, then tilted to the other side.

"There it is!" exclaimed Rebecca as the skimmer straightened out again with a thud. Lights blinked at them out of the darkness. They were flying across water and hadn't realized it because the moon was covered by clouds. "Can you see anywhere to land?"

"I'll put it down as close to the water as possible," whispered Tara, as if they could now hear her. "I can't tell how much land there is on the other side of the buildings but jammer or no jammer I don't want to fly right over them."

"No," shuddered Rebecca, "they would just have to look up to see us."

Tara let the skimmer down near the water's edge. They were only about 400 metres away from the lighted buildings, which they could see through thin forest and bush.

She drove the skimmer right up to the tree line and then manoeuvred in between two thin trees.

"That's good enough," said Rebecca. "We want to be able to get out fast and it'll take us too long to try to get further into the forest. Let's go!"

They jumped out of the skimmer and began their cautious trek toward the Zanu headquarters.

It was very dark. They moved slowly, arms circling so they could feel the trees and bushes, but often tripping over fallen, dead branches. The wind blew strong and hot at their backs. The air had barely cooled off at all. They were both drenched with sweat.

Just as they came to the edge of the bush, the moon came out from behind a cloud. The moonlight, reflected off the huge structure immediately in front of them, seemed so bright that both girls had to shield their eyes. The entire structure, a huge triangle, was made of reflecting glass. Rebecca squinted, trying to see more. There seemed to be two more large triangles attached to the one in front of them, but they angled away in such a manner as to suggest at the very least, a semi-circle of larger triangles.

To Rebecca they looked like giant, modern pyramids, all glaring light and glass. She thought they were at least ten stories high. As she studied them, looking for a way in, a black oval, just the shape of a door, appeared in the glittering wall directly in front of them. Catching Tara's hand, Rebecca ran toward the door, not knowing whether she would find a Zanu guard or Michael. They were almost at the door when a cloud covered the moon. They could see nothing. They couldn't even tell how far they were from the building or where exactly the opening was. With one hand Rebecca clutched Tara's hand so hard that Tara gave a little yelp. Her other hand was extended, groping for the opening. They inched forward. All was black.

Suddenly she and Tara were gripped, together, in a big bear hug. A familiar voice whispered, "See, told you it would be easy."

Michael grabbed each of them by the hand. "This way, and quiet. This is the prisoners' sleeping quarters. And I can tell you, the people here have already denounced their best friends. They'd turn us in without a second thought."

"Where's Rachel?" whispered Rebecca.

"She's gone ahead to the supplies section to see what she can find. Now," he said, whispering so quietly they could barely hear him, "we're in a passageway which leads from the sleeping quarters into the living quarters. That's the big triangle you were standing in front of. From there we'll go through the interrogation centre and into the supply section. We'll keep to the passageway and only enter the building when we get to supply. This is a circle of triangles, each one serving a different function. Beside the supply triangle are the guards' sleeping quarters, then their living quarters, then the stores, and the baths. In the centre of the circle are all their air machines, out in the open. I'm telling you all this in case we get separated. Nowhere is safe. All right, let's not keep Rachel waiting. I'll lead the way. Keep one hand on me, the other on the wall." Rebecca grabbed onto the back of Michael's shirt, Tara clutched the back of Rebecca's top. The passageway could only hold two abreast, so they walked in single file. It was slow going because the passage was pitch black, except for the occasional tiny blue button which glowed out of the darkness on the walls. They hurried along as best they could. Then Michael stopped short. A small red button gleamed in the dark. He pressed it and silently a door slid open. They passed through. He pressed another red button on the other side. The door slid shut. Again they walked on, feeling their way through the dark. There was absolute silence. Rebecca felt they were taking so long—she didn't know if they had been walking for five minutes or an hour. Eventually they passed through another door, then another. Finally Michael stopped before a small blue button on the inner wall. He pressed it. The door opened. They were facing a huge open space, brightly lit. Yellow, styrofoam boxes filled the entire space, row on row, right up to the ceiling. It looked, at first glance, as if they were all suspended in mid-air. But then Rebecca noticed the clear plastic shelves, extending from wall to wall, supporting them. A computer console stood in the centre of the shiny yellow floor. Large robot arms dangled from the shelves, looking like free-floating limbs. One was lowering a box to where Rachel stood, waiting. She turned as she heard them enter.

"Oh," she sighed with relief, "you made it! I've collected a year's supply of water-purifying agents, a year's supply of food pills, and that box has medicines in it."

They saw two large boxes sitting on the floor beside her. The robot arm placed the third box at her feet. She pulled open the flaps and then nodded to the others. "Antibiotics, anti-viral drugs and antiseptics."

"All right," said Michael, "we've got everything. Now let's get out of here."

"Wait! What's that?" said Tara in a terrified whisper.

They could just hear the sound of boots coming down the corridor, closer and closer.

"Hide!" ordered Rachel.

Each of them grabbed a box and dragged it behind the closest line of boxes. Then they ran towards the side walls of the large room. The door opened. They all fell flat where they were.

"What's the light doing on in here?" barked an angry voice.

"Probably Duncan again," responded another voice, this one gruff, tired. "Always trying to make more work for us. As if I don't have enough on my hands—you, you get all the fun work."

"Yeah," laughed the first, "I just sit back and let them babble away into the recorder. I can't complain. But don't think I didn't have to work my way up. I had a full year of disintegrator duty before I got this posting."

"I can't stand listening to all that wailing and moaning," replied the second voice. 'But you said we'd be taken care of!' Some of them fall down, kiss my boots. I zap 'em right away then. Can't stand it. Throw 'em in already dead. 'I am taking care of you!' I say." The voice laughed.

Shivers ran up and down Rebecca's spine.

"We better have a look around here," said the first voice.

"Just to make sure . . . Hey, look at this! The computer's on. Come on—up and down every row."

It was finished. Rebecca sighed. She felt strangely calm now, although her heart was pounding so loudly she could barely hear. They had tried their best—it was all they could have done.

"Don't shoot!" a voice rang out. It was Rachel. She was walking forward, right up to the guards.

"What're you doing in here?" barked one of the guards.

"Exploring," she replied, flippantly.

"A comic! We have a comic here!" said the first voice. "Well, let's see how funny you are in the interrogation unit. March!"

The lights were turned out, the door slid shut and the guards' boots could be heard echoing down the hallway. No one moved until it was silent again. Then Rebecca heard a series of thuds and bumps and after a moment of fright, realized it must be Michael, trying to find the light switch. Finally the lights came back on. Rebecca and Tara stood up, tried to pick up their boxes, but finding them quite heavy, gave up and dragged them towards the door. Michael did the same.

"There must be weapons in here somewhere," Michael said to them, scanning the rows and rows of identical, yellow boxes. "They'll kill her in there, I know they will. We've got to try to get her out."

"But what about the others?" Tara objected. "We could all get caught trying to rescue her—then what?"

Michael looked at Rebecca. "In your day, your vote would be the tie-breaker."

Rebecca looked at them both. Her heart was still pounding from their close call. They had almost been caught. If it hadn't been for Rachel's courage they certainly would have been. Rachel wouldn't want them to come after her.

She'd want them to try to escape, to help the others. How could Rebecca choose?

She bent over and scratched a particularly itchy mosquito bite on her ankle. She thought about what could be happening to Rachel. By the time she'd straightened up she'd made up her mind.

"I can't stand the thought of them hurting her. Let's try to get her out."

Michael grinned. "Good! But we'll need some help. He ran to the computer and punched in the information he wanted. It came up on the screen—where the weapons were stored. He then directed the computer to find them.

They waited as a robot arm slid under a box, and like a miniature fork lift, raised it off the shelf, then lowered it to the floor.

Michael opened it. It was filled with laser weapons. They were small, almost the size and shape of a square pocket flashlight, and were attached to belts. He handed one to Tara and one to Rebecca. He examined them. "You aim, then press the red button," he said. "I ordered stunners, so these shouldn't kill, they should only knock the guards unconscious." They all put on the belts and placed the weapons in the belts. Then they dragged their supplies to the door. Michael opened it. They moved out into the corridor.

"The lights are on now," whispered Rebecca. "Why?"

"The guards probably light the corridors as they make their rounds," Michael replied. "Maybe in the excitement of catching Rachel they forgot to put the lights out. This way," he said, and the girls followed him down the corridor to the door. The supplies were cumbersome. Once they were through the first door, they dragged their boxes to the small blue button on the inner wall, and took out their lasers.

"Ready?" asked Michael. They nodded.

Rebecca noticed that her hand with the weapon in it was shaking. Would she be able to shoot? Or would she be paralyzed? Would she be shot? And would she know she'd been shot before she died?

Michael pressed the blue button. The door opened.

Rachel was seated in a chair directly in front of them. The two guards stood on either side of her. One of them was pointing a small sharp knife at her eye as if he were going to cut her there. Michael shot him and he fell to the floor. Rebecca and Tara both shot at the other, and he, too, fell. All three of them ran to Rachel.

"Rachel, Rachel, are you all right?" asked Tara, hoarsely.

"She is," came a loud male voice from a darkened corner of the room. "But you aren't. Drop your weapons!" They all turned sideways to see a young guard step into the light and point a laser gun at them.

Rebecca thought she could make out a figure sitting in a chair behind the guard but there was too little light to really be certain. "Drop those weapons, I said."

Slowly Tara, then Rebecca dropped their weapons. Rebecca glanced at Michael. He was still holding his. For a moment Rebecca thought he wasn't going to drop it, then she saw his fingers loosen and the gun clattered to the floor.

The guard moved slowly forward, both hands on his laser, pointing it nervously at Michael, then Rachel, then Rebecca, then Tara, trying to keep them all covered.

"A'eeee!" came a huge scream and someone leaped at the guard's back. The person the guard had been interrogating wrapped his arms around the guard's throat, his legs around the guard's waist. The guard fired his weapon, indiscriminately, and laser flashes shot erratically around the room. Then the assailant bent over the guard's neck and bit into it. The guard screamed and dropped his laser. Michael picked up his stunner and ran over to them.

"It's all right," he said to the boy, who was still clinging to the guard, "You can let him go. Don't move," he ordered the guard. The boy, his red hair falling loosely over his face, slid off the guard, who was clutching his bleeding neck. Michael aimed at the guard, and shot. The guard fell to the ground.

Tara's voice filled the room.

"Jonathon! Jonathon! It's my brother!" she proclaimed. Tara ran across the room and hugged him as if she would never let go.

Rebecca could hardly believe her eyes. What was he doing here?

Michael put his hand on Tara's shoulder.

"We've go to go. Now. Your brother can come with us." Beaming, both Jonathon and Tara followed Michael into the hall, but Jonathon had also noticed Rebecca.

"What's she doing here?" he asked. "How . . . ?"

"Never mind," Michael cut him off. "Two of you carry one of those boxes—I can manage one by myself." He hoisted the large box up into his arms. Rachel and Rebecca grabbed one of the others. Jonathon and Tara grabbed the last one. They ran down the corridor until they reached the next door. Instead of pushing the red button leading into the living quarters, however, Michael pressed a small green button on the outer wall. A door slid open. They were facing the night.

Michael led the way out. The wind was blowing so hard now that the force of it almost knocked them all over. Fork lightning crackled around them and a clap of thunder crashed just above their heads.

Tara screamed—and Rebecca was about to get angry with her when she realized that Tara would never have seen

or heard a storm—at any rate her scream was stifled by
the wind and the thunder. Rebecca and Rachel led the way
through the thin forest, battling the wind. The trees were
so brittle that the force of the wind was snapping off
branches, sending bits and pieces flying into their faces.
Rebecca felt a drop of rain on her cheek. Finally, they
reached the skimmer and managed to fit all the boxes into
its storage compartment. Everyone tumbled in, Michael
on the driver's side, Rachel beside him, Rebecca, Tara and
Jonathon in the back.

Michael punched in the coordinates, and the small skimmer rose into the air. The wind buffetted it back and forth,
tilting it to one side, then another and then it was pour-
ing rain, the pellets of water pounding the thin surface of
the craft. Everyone in it was silent.

"I've got to put it down," shouted Michael above the howl
of the storm. "At least until the wind dies down a bit. Let's
just hope we've cleared the water."

He looked at the radar on the screen. "I think there's a
clear spot just below," he shouted. The skimmer tipped
from side to side and bobbed up and down. Then with
a rude jolt they were on the ground, the storm raging
around them.

CHAPTER ELEVEN
The Cave

They sat silently in the skimmer as the storm exploded around them—Michael and Rachel in the front, slumped against the seat in exhaustion; in the back, Tara holding tight to Jonathon's hand, Rebecca hunched over, biting her nails. And she'd worked so hard to stop biting them—but she didn't care anymore. She couldn't help it—she chewed each one down to the skin, slowly, methodically.

Almost without warning, the storm stopped. The rain became a light drizzle, the wind died down.

"What happened?" asked Tara.

"It seems typical of the weather out here," commented Michael. "Very erratic. Storms blow up out of nowhere—and then they're gone." He punched directions into the computer and they lifted off the ground.

"They'll come after us the second they can get their air machines off the ground," he said.

"But they'll be looking all around Zanu headquarters,

won't they?" asked Rebecca. "They don't know we have a skimmer. They'll think we're trying to escape on foot."

"Yes," agreed Michael, "as long as we can get away fast enough so they don't see us. Now, if we can just get back and get the others."

"I hope we're in time for Paul," murmured Tara. She turned to Jonathon.

"Are you all right? Did they hurt you?"

"I'm fine," he said, grinning. "They didn't scare me. I'd *rather* be dead than under their thumb," he added. "But what about you, Tara? And Mother and Father?"

Tara looked at Jonathon for a moment, trying to find the right words. There weren't any right words.

"They've taken Mother and Father. Just after that they came for me but Rebecca and I managed to escape."

"How?" asked Jonathon, bewildered. He looked at Rebecca. "I thought you were safe and sound with Mark," he added, a hint of bitterness in his voice.

"I was, but . . . well . . . "

"But she was so concerned about me that she tried to help and then we found out that Zanu wants to kill her," Tara finished the explanation.

"But why?" asked Jonathon.

"Because after I disappeared with you, there is no record of my being found again," Rebecca answered. "So now they're afraid to let me go back to my time."

Jonathon sat for a moment, absorbing this. When he spoke, his voice was filled with anguish. "Then I ruined everything. If I hadn't gone back to her time, she would have stayed and maybe our time wouldn't be the same."

"Even if that's true," Michael interjected, "we can't say that our time, our present would be better than it is now. Only different. Maybe it was good you brought Rebecca here. Maybe she'll go back and, having seen this future, help change her present so the future *is* better. We can't know. Look on the bright side!" he exclaimed.

As he spoke, he was scanning the small radar screen for any signs of life. He'd set the co-ordinates as close as he could to where he thought the rest of their party was located, but spotting the small group of people was much harder than spotting the huge Zanu complex.

"There they are!" he sighed with relief. Rebecca leaned forward. There on the small screen were four small blips. Within moments the skimmer was on the ground, its light beams illuminating the little cluster of people.

Michael opened the doors and they all poured out and ran to the small group huddled under the trees. Tara scrambled over everyone to reach Paul. He was lying with his head on Sonya's lap, his face wet with fever.

"Paul," said Tara, "I'm back. And I've got some medicine for you. You're going to be fine now."

Paul stared at Tara, but didn't seem to see her.

"Mommy? You home, Mommy?"

Rachel handed Tara two pills and a water flask. "Can you get him to take them?"

"We've got some medicine for you, Paul. Open your mouth wide," said Tara gently. "You must swallow some medicine,"

Paul shook his head and moaned as he twisted from side to side.

Tara licked her forefinger and traced his dry, cracking lips, then slipped her other forefinger and thumb between his lips and placed a pill on his tongue.

"Here, Paul, drink this. Here's some nice, cool water."

Sonya propped up Paul's head and he drank the water and the pill along with it. Tara slipped another pill into his mouth and held the flask to his lips. Paul gulped and sputtered.

"Carry him to the skimmer," said Michael, "We have to go."

They all crowded into the skimmer. This time it was really a tight squeeze. Jonathon, Tara, Rebecca and Kristen in back, with Paul lying across their laps, his head on Jonathon's lap, his feet on Kristen; Michael, Rachel, David and Sonya in the front.

It seemed to take the skimmer longer than usual to lift off, but Rebecca tried to reassure herself that she was imagining this.

"We're very heavy," David's words interrupted her thought, "I hope it can stay afloat."

"We've got to get over the trees, but then what?" Michael said, "Where shall we go?"

There was a temporary silence in the skimmer. Everyone had been so intent on escape, no one had considered where they could establish a camp.

"How should we know?" asked Jonathon, "No one's been here before. One place is as good as the next."

"That's not true," said Rebecca, realizing she had some expertise to offer. "I've been all over Manitoba."

Even David and Sonya turned their heads part way round to look at Rebecca.

She laughed. "You forget that in 1986 we travelled wherever we wanted. I've been to lots of places . . . and I think we should try up North, like around Clear Lake. There are mountains, and it'll be cooler there and maybe we can find some natural shelter. It's just, how'll we find it?"

"Don't worry," answered Michael cheerfully, "just point me in the right direction. I'll find it."

"Well," said Rebecca, trying to remember the map her father always kept in the glove compartment of their car, "it's northeast of Winnipeg, I think."

"Right!" said Michael, and he set the skimmer's co-ordinates.

The pitch black of the night was beginning to give way to grey and over the next hour the sun crept over the horizon. No one in the skimmer saw it, though. They were all fast asleep, exhausted from the night's dangers.

When Rebecca did wake up, it was because Paul was twisting and kicking violently and crying, "Mommy, Daddy, where are you?" She got a sharp kick in the arm before she managed to grasp his legs with both her hands. Jonathon held his arms and Tara stroked his face and tried to soothe him. She gave him more pills and water. Finally he curled up, mostly on Tara, and fell back asleep.

The sun was climbing the sky. It was mid-morning. Below them, green forest clung to small mountains, which surrounded glistening blue-green lakes. Rebecca let out a sigh of pure pleasure at the sight.

"It's wonderful," Tara exclaimed. "It's so beautiful."

"It looks almost the same—although I never saw it from the air," said Rebecca. "It doesn't look like it's been harmed at all."

"Let's set down somewhere," Michael suggested.

"There!" Jonathon pointed at a lovely lake, about a mile by a mile and a half, surrounded by high hills, which sloped gently down to the water.

"Yes," said Rebecca, "I can see some black spots in the hills. They could be caves."

"Once we're out of this skimmer," David cautioned, "their satellites will be able to pick us up. We'll *have* to find a cave or some covering and stay there until we can work out that problem."

"I think," said Michael, frowning, "That I can fix the jamming device so that it will jam all satellite search signals within a small radius of us.

"Really?" said Rebecca, amazed. "You could do that?"

"I think so. After all, they were training me to be a top

programme engineer. I have four years of specialist training. Now, let's see if we can find a big enough cave." He
manoeuvred the skimmer past a few of the dark openings.
One seemed quite large, cut naturally into the face of the
mountain, about halfway up. Michael let the skimmer
hover just in front of it.

"I wonder," he said, "if we can get the whole skimmer
in there?"

"Let me check," suggested Jonathon.

"All right," Michael agreed, manoeuvreing the craft as
close to the opening as he could, and keeping it there,
hovering in the air.

The door slid open and Jonathon leapt from the skimmer onto the ledge of the cave. Within moments of dis-
appearing into the black, he was back on the ledge, wav-
ing Michael in.

"It's fine!" he shouted. "Deep and lots of room."

Michael turned on the beams and eased the skimmer
into the dark cave. The cave seemed to go quite deep into
the mountain, but Michael rested the skimmer close to the
edge. He left the beams on and turned on the interior
lights. They all got out, except Paul and Tara. Tara didn't
want to wake Paul up.

Rebecca looked around.It was a large cave, the roof high,
stretching far back into the mountain. The dirt floor was
smooth and level. And most importantly from Rebecca's
viewpoint, there were no bats. In fact, there seemed to be
no animals or insects of any kind.

"This will do just fine," Michael said, after looking
around. "Our first headquarters. Our first real home," he
proclaimed, grinning from ear to ear. "Now, let's break out
the food and water and have a celebration!"

Rachel opened the storage compartment of the skimmer
and dug around in the boxes until she found a box of food

pills. She handed one to each of them and they passed around what was left of their water.

"We can collect more," Michael said, "as soon as I convert this jamming device."

"Michael," Rebecca interrupted, her voice strained, "I think everyone's forgotten something."

"What's that?" asked Michael.

"If I'm to get home, I'll need to get back to the city and to get back to the city we'll need the jamming device just as it is . . . "

"Of course, Rebecca," said Michael, laughing, "I don't know what I was thinking. Of course, we *have* to get you back—somehow—and right away, I suppose, or everyone here will die of thirst. *No one* can set foot outside of this cave before I readjust this jamming device and you're right, I can't do that until we use it to get you back."

"I'll take her back," said Jonathon.

"What!" Rebecca exclaimed.

"She'll need help. She doesn't know the city, she won't know how to find anything . . . and I got her here. I'm the one to get her back."

"Jonathon!" cried Tara from the skimmer, trying not to jar Paul as she crawled out from under him and out of the skimmer. "You can't! I can't lose you again. I can't. You're the only family I have left."

And then a small voice came from the skimmer, "What about me?"

"Paul!" said Tara, turning back to the skimmer.

Paul looked at them all through the door, his eyes clear, his face calm. He frowned at Tara. "I thought I was your brother," he said. "Who's that?" He pointed to Jonathon.

Tara went back to the skimmer, reached in, pulled Paul out and gave him a huge hug. Then she sat down with him on her lap, her back against the skimmer.

"He's our big brother," she said. "Now you have a sister *and* a brother."

Paul thought about this for a moment, while he looked Jonathon up and down.

"All right," he said, "that's fine, I guess." Then he smiled. "I'm hungry." Tara gave him a big kiss, then took the food pill Rachel handed her and gave it and some water to Paul.

Then they all sat down by the side of the skimmer, its light penetrating the darkness around them, to plan what seemed impossible: how to get Rebecca back to Winnipeg and safely home.

CHAPTER TWELVE
Run and Hide

Rebecca stood in the beams of the skimmer, holding Tara's hands, trying to find the words to say goodbye. This was no ordinary goodbye. This was forever and they both knew it.

The group had quickly come up with a plan—probably because there were so few options open to them. Michael would take Rebecca and Jonathon to the outskirts of Winnipeg at nightfall. He would let them off at a spot where the force field had to be dissolved every few hours for the incoming high-speed trains which transferred people from city to city. Michael, having worked on all facets of programming, knew where these entered and exited. David and Sonya had instructed Jonathon to take Rebecca to their home—they knew their children were sympathetic and would help. Once all that had been decided, there was nothing left but to wait. They sat around, talked and dozed. Jonathon was carefully instructed on the new camp's co-ordinates. These he was to pass on to the anti-Zanu forces, so they could send people to the camp who were in danger of being cut loose.

Finally it was time to go.

"I hope you find your parents, Tara," said Rebecca, squeezing Tara's hand. "And your sister. Try not to worry too much about Jonathon. He'll come back to you. He's so tough nothing will stop him."

Tara looked at Rebecca, her eyes filled with tears. "Be careful," she said, "and get home safely."

Rebecca nodded. She and Tara hugged each other. Rebecca bent and gave Paul a kiss on the head. "No more swimming in the lake," she cautioned him with mock severity.

He laughed. "But maybe the water is nice here. It looks so pretty."

"It just may be," David agreed. "But you'll let us test it *first*, won't you Paul?"

Paul drew a circle in the dirt with his toe. "I guess so," he conceded.

Rebecca said goodbye to everyone then and climbed into the skimmer.

Tara threw her arms around Jonathon's neck and clung to him. Finally, she loosened her grip and forced herself to back away. She gave him a big smile, and said, "See you soon."

Rebecca thought it was the bravest thing she'd seen Tara do. Jonathon climbed into the front seat beside Rebecca and they were off. The blackness surrounded them. For a few short hours they would be relatively safe—but once on the ground, satellites would be able to detect their presence, Zanu guards could track them—they would need a lot of luck to make it safely to David's house. Rebecca thought about home—about Lewis and Catherine, her friends Marta and Lonney. Would she ever get a chance to tell them about this? Probably they were all worried sick. Her parents would probably have been on TV, appealing to supposed kidnappers to return their daughter safely. The plea would certainly fall on deaf ears at Zanu headquarters—if they could hear it. They wanted her dead, at any cost, and she was afraid she might be walking into their arms.

As if reading her mind, Jonathon said, "Don't worry! They won't catch us. Know why? We're smarter than those . . . those . . ."

"Goons," Rebecca suggested.

"I don't know what that means," laughed Michael, "but I love the sound of it. Goons. Fits them perfectly."

They flew in silence, for the most part, too aware of the danger ahead to feel like talking.

Rebecca found herself thinking about the world she was returning to, the Zanu world—where no one had the right to be different, where no one could choose anything for themselves except what things to buy. Was that happening already in her present? She knew that there were many countries in her world where people had no freedom at all. But somehow, she'd never thought it could happen in Winnipeg. Was it happening already? Was everyone so concerned about making money that no one would stop the pollution because that would lose them their jobs, their profits? Her thoughts were interrupted when a shimmering wall glowed at them through the blackness. It was faint at first but grew stronger and brighter.

Michael flew almost up to the force field, then parallel to it. When he found the right spot, he set the skimmer down.

"We've timed it almost perfectly," he said. "In a few minutes the train will come along and the force field will be lowered directly ahead of us. I'm going to open the doors now, but you must stay in the skimmer until the force field drops. Then run straight from here into the city. That way the satellites probably won't pick you up. And then get out of the way of the train!"

"What about you?" asked Rebecca. "Can you get out of the way fast enough?"

"Of course!" Michael laughed. "Don't worry about me." He paused. "We'd better say goodbye now." He looked at Rebecca. "I'll miss you. In a way, I wish you could stay and help us."

Rebecca felt herself blushing. "I'll do my best to get back home and help you that way."

Michael looked at Jonathon. "Be careful, Jonathon," he warned. "Don't take any unnecessary chances. Don't let that temper of yours get the best . . . It's happening! The force field is dissolving. Get ready."

Rebecca and Jonathon braced themselves. The shimmer in front of them began to evaporate, then disappear. A clear, large oval space appeared in front of them and they could hear the distant hum of the train coming from behind them.

"Go!" yelled Michael.

They pushed themselves out of the skimmer, Jonathon first, then Rebecca. They ran for their lives. The hum of the train was getting louder. Rebecca realized they were running on the track. It wasn't like the train tracks she knew. It was flat and wide and black and hard. Perhaps it was magnetic, she thought, and the train sped along just over its surface. However it travelled, she knew they would soon be seen in the glare of its lights.

"Jump!" Rebecca yelled, and leapt off the track. She landed on her hands and feet, flattened herself to the ground and felt herself rolling downhill. Then Jonathon was tumbling over her and they were in the bottom of a ditch. The train whizzed past, and within a minute, was gone. Everything was quiet. Rebecca, lying flat on her stomach, raised her head and looked up and around. Jonathon rolled into a crouch.

"Who would ever have thought," Rebecca muttered, "that one day people would be forced to run and hide like scared animals—right here in Winnipeg!"

"They won't! Not if I can help it!" exclaimed Jonathon, his eyes burning.

Suddenly they heard the quiet hum of a skimmer. Rebecca's heart began to pound. Jonathon turned whiter than usual. They pressed themselves flat in the bottom of the ditch and held themselves motionless.

The skimmer hummed by. They began to relax. Moments later they heard another hum. It was very close.

"I think Zanu's probably patrolling the area," Jonathon whispered. "Maybe the train driver reported seeing something. We'll have to keep to the back lanes and move as fast as we can." He crawled up the side of the ditch. "I don't see anything. Let's go!"

Rebecca, too, clambered out of the ditch and they ran towards the nearest back lane. It was horrible trying to run in the dark, never knowing what they could trip over or bump into, but they had no choice. Jonathon led them down the lanes. He counted as they went, to give them a sense of the street numbers. Everything was quiet. No one was out on the streets.

Suddenly he held out his hand. They stopped. A Zanu guard skimmer whizzed by, about fifty metres in front of them, just as they were coming to a main street. It continued on its way, however, and Rebecca and Jonathon, hearts pounding, ran across the street into another back lane.

"Not far now," said Jonathon. "As we crossed back there I saw the sign 440 St. N. Five more blocks and we're there."

Rebecca counted as they ran. And then, finally, Jonathon was counting houses. "One, two, three, four—here it is," he gasped. "No. 5" They ran up to the back window, crouched, and Jonathon knocked gingerly on the window pane. The house was dark—it was well past midnight. No one stirred. He knocked more loudly. Again nothing. "If we ring the door chimes," he whispered, "the computer will record a late-night visitor. Why don't they wake up?" he said, beginning to get frustrated.

Rebecca, every muscle in her body a tense knot, her eyes darting everywhere, was watching for Zanu skimmers. Finally, she could stand it no longer and pounded on the glass with the flat of her hand.

"Shshsh!" Jonathon grabbed her wrist.

"Well, which is worse? This noise or waiting to get caught by a Zanu patrol?" she hissed.

Suddenly they noticed a pair of eyes staring at them through the glass. Then another pair. Then the eyes disappeared. And within a few moments a young man and a young woman were standing on either side of them. They towered over Rebecca and Jonathon.

"What do you want?" whispered the young woman.

"We were sent here by David and Sonya," Jonathon replied. "They said you'd help us."

"Why should we believe them?" the young man said to the woman. "This could be some kind of trap."

"Look," said Rebecca. "We've risked a lot to get here. They said you'd help us, and we need help."

"Who are you?" asked the young woman.

"I'm Rebecca," she replied. "And this . . . "

"Wait!" said the woman. "Are you the child from the past?"

"Why, yes," Rebecca replied. "How did you know . . . ?"

"Never mind that," she replied. "Come in, both of you. Follow me straight to my bedroom. We've fixed it so it's safe from that prying computer."

She led the way into the house, through the darkened main room, down the steps, and into her brightly lighted room. She was extremely tall, Rebecca saw, as was her brother. Both had long blond hair and green-grey eyes. They were very striking.

"Are you . . . " Rebecca looked from one to the other. "Are you . . . "

"Twins. Yes," she replied. "I'm Susan, this is Gary. You're Rebecca, and this is . . . "

"Jonathon."

"How are my parents?" Susan asked anxiously.

"We think they're fine," Rebecca answered. "They're hiding up north. We've set up a camp . . . " Suddenly there was a buzzing in her ears, her legs seemed to crumple beneath her and she fell against the foot of the bed.

"We haven't eaten much, and we haven't slept much . . . and we've been running . . . " Jonathon explained.

Susan sat down beside Rebecca. "Let's get some blood to your head," she suggested, as she raised Rebecca's knees and gently pressed her head down.

Rebecca found she was panting, her breath coming in erratic gasps.

Susan and Peter looked at them. They were in a terrible state. Their clothes were torn and filthy, their hair matted, and their faces drawn with fatigue.

"Look," said Susan. "You can tell us everything later. How would you like a hot shower, some fresh clothes and a great big hot supper?"

"Yes," Rebecca sighed. "Please."

"Follow me," Susan said to Rebecca and led her to the

bathroom. "There's a set of clothes hanging on the hook. Just get into those."

"Thanks," said Rebecca, and she slipped into the bathroom. She took off all her clothes, threw them in a pile and stepped into the shower stall. Little sprays of soap coated her. Then the water hit her from all sides. She rubbed her hair clean. Then a blast of hot air dried her off. She got dressed. She had to roll the pant legs up about five times, and the sleeves, but at least the clothes were clean. They were rather like long black silk pyjamas. She found a brush and did her hair.

By the time she rejoined the others she felt wonderful— but very lightheaded from hunger.

Jonathon then took his turn and Rebecca plunked herself down on the bed. Susan had put a tray on a small, round, clear plastic table. She pushed the table right up to the bed.

"You'd better eat something," she advised. Rebecca dug into what looked like a real piece of meat, and real vegetables, but which tasted tart.

"Kelp," said Gary.

She was drinking a Coke when Jonathon came into the bedroom, clean and dressed in some of Gary's clothes— also with pants and sleeves rolled up. He ate, then they both sank against the bed, on the thick grey carpet, ready to answer questions.

"Your parents are fine," said Rebecca. "Better than could be expected, really."

"What do you mean by that?" asked Gary.

"Just that if we hadn't escaped they'd probably be dead soon—now at least they have a chance." She paused. "Look. I'd better tell you from the beginning, or at least what I know."

Rebecca recounted how she had come to their world, her meeting with David and Sonya, and all the events right up until she and Jonathon knocked on their window.

"And you," Gary said to Jonathon when Rebecca had finished, "are hoping we'll help you set up some kind of underground."

"Yes," said Jonathon gravely.

"Pretty dangerous work, don't you think?"

"Yes."

The twins grinned at each other, then beamed at Jonathon and Rebecca.

Susan laughed aloud and then explained. "We've already begun! You've come to the right place. We already have a system of bypassing the Zanu frequencies and we're co-ordinating all the anti-Zanu forces from a safe house. We've set up a series of safe houses all over the city, so that people who suspect they're about to be cut loose can go underground instead. Now that you have this hideout established up north, people will have a second option—they can make their way up there by sneaking out of the city the same way you snuck in."

Jonathon was stunned.

"I can't believe it! Why, you're doing exactly what I had planned . . . "

"There are more people than you realize, Jonathon," said Gary, "who feel the same way we do. And now that we know that the disintegrator isn't just used for objects, I think more and more will join us."

"Can I stay here?" Jonathon asked.

"Of course," Susan replied. "But I'm afraid you'll be terribly restricted. And it's not right for a young boy like you to be stuck in one room day after day!"

"It doesn't matter," replied Jonathon. "At least I'm free here, I'm not being re-educated or disintegrated, and I can do something to help."

"And now it's our job to get Rebecca back to her time,"

said Susan. "When?" she mused. "And how? It won't be easy. The first thing we have to do is to find out about the security on the time machine, and then plan a strategy with our people. We'll do that in the morning. But now you'll have to be moved."

"What!" exclaimed Rebecca and Jonathon together.

"Yes, you'll have to be moved," repeated Susan. "This house is not safe. Because of our parents, we're high risk— we're watched constantly. While you were cleaning up I contacted someone—they're going to pick you up and take you to the safe house."

Just then they heard a faint scratching against the wall.

"He's here," Gary said.

"Right," said Susan. "We may not see you again. You'll be safe where you're going. Do *exactly* as you're told and we'll all hope for the best. You'll have to travel in the storage compartment. Just run out to the skimmer, jump in and the top'll be fastened down." She held out her hand to each of them.

"Good luck," she said as they shook hands.

"Good luck," Gary echoed as he, too, held out his hand. "Follow me," he said.

He led them out of Susan's bedroom, up the steps, through the darkened central area to the front door, which slid open. They could just make out the skimmer waiting for them in the street. They ran to it, then hopped into the storage area in the back. Rebecca tried to see their escort but it was too dark. Someone closed the compartment and they were moving.

It seemed like hours, but Rebecca knew it was probably no more than ten minutes later when the door was opened and a voice said, "Here we are. Run to the house. I'll close up after you."

They leaped out and ran from the back to the front of

the house. Their escort put his hand on a milky square; it glowed red, the door opened. They hurried inside. It was dark. They waited.

"Follow me," the voice said.

"That's strange," Rebecca thought. "That voice . . . I'd swear I've heard it . . . "

He led them into the central area, then pushed the button on the floor. The floor panel slid back. He almost pushed them down the unlit stairs.

"Careful!" Rebecca complained. "We'll kill ourselves." Cautiously she felt her way down the stairs. When they were all down, he pushed the wall button. The bedroom door slid open and bright light flooded the hallway.

"Mark!" both Rebecca and Jonathon exclaimed at the same time.

He pushed them into the bedroom and pushed the button to shut the door. He turned to them and smiled. "I thought I'd never see either of you again."

"But . . . but . . . " Jonathon was quite speechless.

"I've been working against Zanu since my eleventh birthday, Jonathon," Mark said, plopping himself onto the bed.

"But . . . then why . . . why did you . . . "

"Why did I go after you? Well, I didn't have much time to think it over—I just felt that you might start things which we couldn't control. At least we were developing ways to fight here—you could have made things better—or worse."

"And I did make them worse—I somehow did just what history says I did—managed to spirit Rebecca away . . . " said Jonathon. "Maybe the future's all set," he added, "and we're just doing what we have to do . . . "

"Maybe," Mark said. "But if we can get Rebecca back, then we know that's not so."

"But . . . " said Jonathon, "I always thought you were all for Zanu . . . "

"I couldn't tell you, Jonathon," said Mark. "You were too unpredictable. We were afraid you'd do something rash, get us and yourself into trouble."

For a moment the two friends just looked at each other. Rebecca thought she understood what was going on. They had been best friends, had lost each other, then found they were even closer than they thought. Mark got off the bed and went up to Jonathon. Soon they were hugging, laughing and hugging again.

Rebecca beamed at them both.

"You certainly fooled me," she said to Mark.

"I had to," he tossed back. "It's my cover."

"Then . . . it was you who tipped people off—who helped Tara and me escape."

Mark nodded. "Tell me what happened," he said.

They all lay on the bed, their heads together in the centre, and Rebecca told him what had happened to her and Tara since leaving in the middle of the night. He listened with great interest. As she drew near the end of her story, Jonathon began to tell Mark what had happened to him after he had been cut loose. Rebecca crawled under the covers of the bed. Mark and Jonathon's voices began to drift to her from farther and farther away. It was three A.M. and she hadn't slept for . . . how long? She was too tired to figure it out. The bed was so wonderful, the sheets were silky and cool, the comforter light but warm. Idly she wondered if it was a waterbed—or maybe it was made of air? That was her last thought before she fell into a deep, much-needed sleep.

CHAPTER THIRTEEN
A Time to Travel

Rebecca opened her eyes. She was lying in a strange bed in a strange room and for a moment she really couldn't remember where she was. Somehow, though, she knew she was glad to be in a real bed and to be smelling real food . . . Oh! She sat up. Mark was entering the room, a tray in his hand. He set it down on a small, round, clear plastic table beside the bed. He smiled.

"Good morning. Did you sleep well?"

"I . . . I . . . guess I did," Rebecca replied. She looked at the food and the drink, steam rising from the cup. "What is it?" she asked.

"Toasted kelp bread, artificial fruit and tea," grinned Mark.

"Oh . . . " Rebecca tried to look enthusiastic. "*Real* tea?"

"*Real* tea, and very rare, I might add. I thought you might enjoy it." He sat down on the edge of the bed.

The toast was edible, if tart, the fruit tasted slightly bitter, and the tea was quite lovely and hot. All in all, after her experience up north, it was a wonderful breakfast.

"Where's Jonathon?" she asked, as she drank the last of her tea.

"Just finishing breakfast in my room," Mark said. "I've told him to come in here when he's dressed and ready—it's almost 11 A.M. and our people have been very busy planning your escape. Everything is arranged."

"Already?"

"Yes. The longer you're here the greater the chances are you'll be caught. I've already been out and bought clothes for you and Jonathon. Naturally Jonathon will have to stay here, in hiding, for the moment. You will be picked up by Kevin at 11:30. He'll drive you to the museum, where the time machine is kept. It's under *very* heavy guard since Jonathon and I used it, but we've planned a diversion and we'll be armed. Kevin has the co-ordinates you'll need to program the time machine so it will get you home, but so do at least five others, should things get rough. Your job is to get yourself into that machine. And home. Somehow, then, history as we know it will change . . . " he paused. "What, I wonder, will that mean?"

Rebecca looked at him thoughtfully. "Do you think you could all be—sorry about this, but—wiped out in that one second when I get home?"

She hoped he would laugh, tell her she was being over-imaginative. But he didn't.

"It's possible," he said.

"But then *why* are you so anxious to send me back? I could stay, and we could change things here. I don't want to be responsible for wiping out billions of people!"

Now he did smile, a little.

"I only said possible. After all, how should I know. Probably we'll all be here—but maybe something you do in your future will change our present . . . or maybe just the fact of your changing our history will cause all sorts of different possibilities."

"Different strands on the fan . . . " Rebecca mused.

"Yes," agreed Mark. "We all feel it's a chance we'll have to take." Again he paused for a moment. "The only thing that really bothers me," he said finally, "is that if things do change radically the second you get back to your world —we probably won't know the difference. All of a sudden we'll be the same people but with different histories and we won't remember any of this."

"Or me," Rebecca said softly.

"Or you," Mark admitted.

"And," Rebecca was getting agitated, "I'll never know what happened to everyone here . . . "

"Of course, there is one other possibility," Mark interrupted.

"What?"

"Nothing will change."

"But even if my going back doesn't change things, you'll change things," Rebecca said. "I know you will. Now that you have a base up north and people here working . . . "

"Well," said Mark. "Nothing will happen if we sit here all day. I've got to get you ready. They'll be here for you any minute! Your clothes are hanging in the bathroom. Don't go into the central living quarters; the computer will pick you up."

When Rebecca returned to the bedroom, washed and dressed in her new clothes—a shocking pink silk suit— Jonathon and Mark were waiting for her.

"Kevin is outside," said Mark. "Just walk out to the skimmer and get in. Act as naturally as you can."

Rebecca looked at them both and hesitated. She had been desperate to get home ever since she arrived, but suddenly everything seemed to be happening too fast.

"You have to go *now*," said Mark.

Rebecca knew he was right. Impulsively she kissed Mark and Jonathon on the cheek, then, without a word, left the bedroom, walked along the wall to the outer door, and let herself out.

A small red skimmer hovered just above the road, right in front of the house. She forced herself to walk calmly down the sidewalk and get into the skimmer without undue haste. Her teeth had begun to chatter again.

"Hello," said a small young man with curly dark hair and dark eyes. "Ready?"

She nodded and attempted a smile. It was difficult with her teeth chattering.

They drove down the street towards the centre of town. They were just entering the busy section of the city when a Zanu guard skimmer pulled up beside them and motioned them to stop.

"Keep calm," said Kevin under his breath, as two Zanu guards approached their windows, one on either side.

Kevin pushed the controls and the windows rolled down. "Routine I.D. check," said the guards.

Rebecca's heart, already pounding in her head so hard she could barely hear, seemed to sink and sink. She turned cold with fear. She sat, hands in her lap, and tried not to shake. Any show of fear would make them suspicious. She shut her mouth tightly so her teeth wouldn't chatter.

"Certainly," Kevin said, smiling. He reached for a small compartment on the front of the skimmer. As he did so, Rebecca saw his hand stray to the computer. Suddenly the skimmer rocketed forward and away from the stunned guards. Rebecca looked behind her. They were drawing their weapons but Kevin already had the skimmer turning a corner and racing down a side street. They were entering into the busy part of town at a tremendous speed, passing other skimmers, almost running people down as they moved over sidewalks when necessary.

Then, on a very busy shopping street, Kevin said, "We've got to dump the skimmer and walk now. Get out. We'll lose ourselves in the crowd."

They both got out of the skimmer and walked into the thick of the jostling crowds. Kevin grasped Rebecca's hand tightly.

"Not too fast, now," he cautioned. "Don't want to draw any attention to ourselves."

He pulled her through the crowds until finally they were climbing the museum steps. They walked through the exhibit rooms and into the huge display room which housed the time machine. At first sight, it reminded Rebecca of an igloo. It even had a long, rounded, igloo-like entrance leading into it. All around it, along the walls of the huge room, were displays of various kinds of housing—tents, caves, grass huts, miniature brick buildings, log cabins. Teachers and their students were milling around them.

Rebecca stayed as close to Kevin as she could, watching his every move. She saw him nod, but couldn't see who he was nodding to. Someone must have seen his signal, though, because suddenly the grass hut and log cabin were in flames, and people were screaming and running in all directions. Some of the guards left their posts around the time machine, but most stood their ground and jerked to attention, lasers ready. In the next moment, however, they all crumpled to the floor. Amidst the panic, the anti-Zanu people had each taken one guard, aimed their weapons, then on a signal from Kevin, fired.

Kevin pulled Rebecca forward. Rebecca saw laser flashes all around them. Obviously, more guards were converging on the room and the anti-Zanu forces were having to fight them off.

Kevin and Rebecca ducked into the long, white tunnel. A huge computer console was built into one of its walls. They ran alongside it toward a door at the far end of the tunnel. Kevin pressed a button on the wall and the door slid up.

"Get in!" Kevin ordered. "Quick!"

"But what about you?" asked Rebecca.

"Never mind! We have an escape plan. Now go!" Kevin commanded, his finger on the button for the door.

Rebecca stepped back into the central compartment of the time machine. Kevin pushed the button, then dashed to the computer console. The white door slid down, then everything was deathly quiet.

Was she imagining it, or was she having that strange sensation again, the sensation of the world going soft.

"Do you need some help, young lady?"

Black boots! Rebecca's heart sank. She looked up. A young policeman was standing right beside her. She was lying . . . where? She sat up and looked around. She was in the park. Near the duck pond.

"Yes. Yes, I do," she said weakly.

The policeman helped her up.

"What, what time is it?" she asked.

"Nine o'clock."

"And what day?"

The way he looked at her made Rebecca realize she shouldn't have asked that.

"July 6," he said. "And now perhaps you should come along to police headquarters."

"No, no," she said, trying to pull herself together. "I was here with my family, officer, and, well, I must've fallen when I was running, and hit my head . . . please, just take me home."

He looked at her doubtfully.

"All right, young lady. Home first, then we'll see."

He pointed to a police cruiser, parked on the road which wound past the duck pond.

"Into the back and buckle up," he ordered, opening the door for her.

She sat down in the back seat and did up her seat belt. She couldn't help but think of the other police car and a much different kind of seat belt. She could still hear the whirring noise it made and how it had snapped shut around her.

"Can I open the window?"

"Sure."

The soft, warm air caressed her skin. The sun was setting and the sky was a mass of purple, blues, pinks, and oranges. She could smell freshly cut grass and flowers. She breathed deeply. She was about to cry, when the officer said, looking over his shoulder at her, "That's some outfit you got on there!"

"You should only know where I got it!" she replied, in a cascade of laughter and tears.

He shook his head.

"Well, let's get you home," he said. "See what your parents have to say about all this."

"Yes," agreed Rebecca. "Just get me home."

Our Fifth Perception series presents action-packed science fiction/adventure stories dealing with contemporary issues.